The
Sins of
Rachel
Ellis

Philip Caveney

The Sins of Rachel Ellis

St. Martin's Press
New York

For My Parents
And for Charlie, without whom . . .

Prologue

EXTRACT FROM THE JOURNAL OF ALEX ELLIS (1862–1910):

January 7th, 1910
Carmarthen, South Wales

The weight of my guilt has become unbearable. I am determined to hesitate no longer. I realise now that I am neither callous enough nor heartless enough to claim the gift that could so easily be mine. It is now only four weeks since I took the boy; and my initial transference was a spectacular success; but the child paces to and fro up in that little room and sometimes screams aloud in the night, such a lonely pleading sound. Damn me for being nothing but a weak-hearted fool. A thousand times I have bid myself be at ease but each time my conscience gets the better of me.

My will is made up and ready (though I think it will cause some raised eyebrows when it is read)! I have bequeathed the house and the Goblin charm to my young niece, Rachel. I have met her but once, some ten years ago and I fancy that if anyone has the cold-blooded temperament required to make full use of my discovery, it is she; I am nothing if not a mean judge of character.

It is late and I have drunk much wine. I can hear him moving up there, stumbling and moaning. Lord, what a sound! May God forgive me for what I have done. . . .

I do not know what I am to expect but I go now, with good heart and sound mind, to free him from his prison.

No further entries were made.

EXTRACTS FROM THE DIARY OF MISS RACHEL ELLIS:

January 24th, 1912
Savannah, Georgia

What strange wayward spirit has hold of me? I declare, never have I been so obsessed with a single idea in my life, than I am now over the matter of the legacy. It is about two years since I first learned of Uncle Alex's will. Though I was amazed and delighted by his kindness then and have always worn the cute little silver charm around my neck, I have never before had the slightest inclination to take up residence in my house in Gt Britain.

Why suddenly, do I find myself *itching* to visit the place, even though I have never seen it in my life? There is a powerful restlessness in me. I feel myself drawn to those distant shores, like a moth to a candle flame. I am sure of one thing. I must go there and soon, if I am ever to regain any peace of mind.

January 26th, 1912

I told Mama and Papa of my intentions this evening. They were amazed and I think, somewhat upset at my desire to leave home. At first Papa was set against the notion; and all Mama could say was that I was only a baby! I explained to them calmly that I intended to visit my British home, with or without their permission and that as for being a baby, I would indeed look a sorry sight in bib and bonnet at the age of twenty-two!

Eventually, I managed to talk them round. Papa agreed to book passage for me on one of the ocean liners out of New York and he said that I might take whichever maid that I choose along with me as a companion.

Once again I find myself wondering about Uncle Alex. I remember meeting him but once, here in Savannah, when I was around ten years old. He was a strange, genial man, very fond of the drink; my parents always thought him rather vulgar. I recall that he was very taken with me and was always stroking my hair and sitting me on his knee; he would talk to me for hours, though of course my memories are all very vague as to exactly what he said to me. There was something about "recognising" me; or perhaps, a quality in me. . . . It really was a very long time ago.

January 27th, 1912

Last night I had a terrible dream. It was quite the most vivid, perplexing dream I can ever remember having and it was obviously linked with my excitement about the coming journey. To begin with I seemed to be whizzing through the air at a tremendous speed, over a barren mountainous landscape. After a few moments, I saw before me, in the near distance, a big mansion house of dark grey stone, half obscured by a screen of trees. In the air above this house, there hovered a gigantic red book which cast a great oblong shadow over the building.

As I drew nearer my gaze was drawn to a large window on the ground floor of this house; inside, at a writing desk sat a familiar figure, that of Uncle Alex. He seemed to be trying to read; but every now and then, he would glance upwards as though aware of something above him. There was great apprehension in his face, a look of dread.

Abruptly, the scene changed. I was lying in a four-poster bed in a gloomy, unfamiliar room; a room, I felt sure, that was in the same mansion that I had seen earlier.

I peered around me and could dimly make out several items of furniture and directly in front of me, a door. Just as I became aware of this, it began to creak slowly open. I watched intently.

Into the room came a small, naked boy. His face and body were of a ghastly white pallour, contrasting with his black shoulder-length hair. Where his eyes should have been, there was nothing, only two empty sockets. To my own amazement, I felt no fear at his presence.

He began to beckon to me, a curious smile upon his lips. After a moment's hesitation, I slipped out of bed and followed him back out through the doorway. He led me down a long, creaking corridor, his body seeming to glide along the floor, so that I was obliged to hurry to keep up. Next, we went down a flight of stairs, then another. A hallway lay before us. The boy did not hesitate. He hurried along the length of the hall and slipped into a doorway to his right. I raced after him, determined not to let him escape.

As I went through the door, the boy turned to face me. I stopped, gazed around the room. It was comfortably furnished and the walls were lined with bookshelves. At the far end of the room, a huge stone fireplace dominated and in the grate, a low fire still smouldered. The boy stretched out a thin white arm and pointed to the bare wall above the mantle. I stared at it and saw that the wall was extremely damp; in fact, as I watched, this condition began to grow rapidly worse. The plaster seemed to become moist and decayed. Pieces flaked off and fell into the hearth at an astonishing rate and after a few moments, I perceived a square alcove within the wall itself. Standing inside this was a tattered red book; an exact replica of the huge volume that I had observed floating above the house.

I turned back to face the boy, intending to ask him something, and saw to my horror, that his face had taken on the very likeness of the mouldering wall. His flesh was collapsing upon itself and dropping away to reveal the skull beneath.

I awoke screaming.

January 28th, 1912

I have thought very deeply these last two days about the dream and its possible implications. I have considered that it may be a premonition of danger, I have considered that it may be a warning. Whatever it was, it has only served to intrigue me more than ever; I *have* to go to Uncle Alex's house. I may live to regret this decision, but I am convinced that I am doing the right thing.

Part
The First

The
Goblin
Tree

Chapter One

Paddington station resembled an ant hill.

Beneath the great dusty glass roof, countless numbers of people scurried to and fro in the bleak morning. They queued impatiently for tickets; they hurried along grey platforms; they slammed train doors, or leaned from windows, waving and shouting. Some of them struggled beneath the weight of bulky suitcases. Yet more waited upon their appropriate platforms, half hidden behind newspapers. Everywhere there was a great coming and going, a feeling of urgency. It was Monday morning and there were appointments to keep, wages to earn and little time for indulging in pointless conversation.

Pandora sat upon an uncomfortable bench, feeling small; as small as only a twelve-year-old child can, when she is within minutes of leaving her parents for the summer. She gazed wistfully along the rails to where they converged in the distance and her heart was already gone, a million miles down that lonely track. Then she glanced back anxiously towards the newsagent's kiosk, where her Mother was waiting in line.

Pandora wished that she could turn around and call the whole thing off. There was a vague feeling of unease within her, a certain something that didn't really make sense; after all, she herself had engineered this leaving. She had wanted to help. She still wanted to help.

A train pulled into the station, disturbing her thoughts. It clattered dismally to a halt.

Samantha hurried over with the comics.

"These are the only ones they had, darling. I hope they're O.K."

Pandora smiled. "They'll be fine, Mummy. Don't worry."

They exchanged a brief glance. Samantha's eyes were inscrutable behind the dark glasses that she always wore. She sat down beside her daughter. "Is this your train?" she inquired.

Pandora shrugged. "I think so. But there's ten minutes yet. No hurry."

"Well, we've got to get your trunk on yet . . . oh dear, are you *sure* you want to go through with this. . . ?"

"Of course." Pandora grinned. "You make it sound awful."

"It's not that. It's just . . . well, I don't want you to feel that we're trying to get rid of you."

"Mummy! Don't be silly. I want to go."

"Do you, dear? Really?"

"It'll be fun."

"Fun. Yes. . . ."

"*Really.*"

Samantha nodded, smiled. She seemed reassured. Pandora wished that her Mother would take off the sunglasses; she would have liked to see her eyes. But that, of course was impossible. She would almost certainly be recognised as Samantha West, Film Star, and the indifferent crowd that thronged the station would become fans; a dangerous, predatory breed. Pandora had seen it happen a couple of times and she despised it. She hated seeing her Mother trapped and helpless in the midst of a mob, whose only ambition was to snatch a small part of her away.

So the glasses stayed on, Samantha's only protection against a hungry world.

"She *needs* protection," thought Pandora. "Daddy's always so wrapped up in his books. . . ."

"Oh, there's a porter now," exclaimed Samantha. "Excuse me!"

The man slouched over as though he was carrying the world on his narrow shoulders. There was an expression of acute boredom on his face. He eyed Pandora's large trunk suspiciously.

"Yes, love?"

"Could you put this in the guard's van please? Oh, this is the Swansea train, isn't it?"

He glanced sleepily behind him as though he'd been unaware of the train's existence till now. "Uh . . . oh yeah, that's the one."

"Fine. Here you are." She pressed a pound note into his hand and he brightened up instantly.

"Thank you, Mam!" He hurried off to collect his trolley.

"Let's find you a compartment," suggested Samantha. She picked up the little suitcase and the two of them strolled over to the train. Pandora pulled herself aboard and wrinkled her nose disdainfully at the smell of warm dust and urine. She led the way along the corridor until they found a vacant compartment. They went in and Samantha stowed the suitcase up above.

"I wish I was travelling with you," she sighed. "Now don't forget. . . ."

"Change at Swansea! Yes, I know."

"And try to get on with Great Aunt Rachel, won't you. Remember she's very old, so she won't want a barrage of noise night and day. . . ."

"I'll brush my teeth after every meal," promised Pandora with a grin.

Samantha shook her head ruefully. She gazed down at this strange twelve-year-old creature that just happened to be her daughter. Pandora was by no means a beautiful child, but there was a certain tomboyish attraction to her. Her face was elf-like, the features small and delicate. Her eyes were quite striking, wide and blue, they surveyed the world with quiet confidence, from either side of a tiny snub nose. Her hair was a confusion of copper-coloured waves, that fell down to her shoulders in an unruly tangle, framing the quick intelligence of her face. She looked a trifle uncomfortable in the white blouse and plain black skirt that her Mother had made her wear. She had always preferred the less formal attire of jeans and T-shirt. Beneath the cotton fabric of the blouse, her breasts were surprisingly full for her age, though she had not yet accepted the need for a bra. Her white stockingless legs looked somehow awkward, splayed as they were against the dusty seat.

"She's growing up," thought Samantha, vaguely. "She seems to grow another inch every time I turn around. . . ."

She was suddenly reminded of an old joke.

Parent. "It's about time we discussed the facts of life."

Child. "Certainly Mummy. . . . What did you want to know?"

Whoever originated that little gem probably had Pandora in mind, or at least, someone very much like her. It wasn't that she was a precocious kid . . . no, it was something harder to define than that. Pandora had an aura about her that spoke of knowledge far in excess of her tender years, a sort of quiet self-assured confidence that twelve-year-old children did not, as a rule, possess. Of course she'd always been an independent little so and so; but then, she'd had to be. She probably had the worst possible combination of parents, an actress and an author. It was a volatile mixture.

Samantha was totally caught up in making movies. It had always been her true love, taking precedence over her social and family life. Hence, much of Pandora's childhood had been spent in airport lounges, waving good-bye as her Mother jetted away to perform in front of movie cameras on the other side of the world.

Her Father's work, on the other hand, kept him constantly at home. John Ellis was a pretty successful novelist, the author of over fifteen books, two of them best sellers; but it was a success that he had earned by long hours alone in his room, with a notepad and typewriter. Maybe it was his ability to live so vividly on paper that had stifled the reality of his life and made him the strange, brooding, secretive man that he was.

All in all, it was amazing that the marriage had survived as long as it had. On the rare occasions that John and Samantha were together, they invariably argued and bickered about stupid, shallow little differences. More recently, the confrontations had become increasingly physical and the marriage was all but hanging in shreds. What had once been merely verbal abuse had lately degenerated into out and out violence. All too often, Pandora had been awakened by the sound of breaking ornaments in her parents' bedroom, a noise that was invariably followed by her Mother's hysterical crying or her Father's incensed yells. Perhaps Pandora was the one factor that kept the marriage clinging together.

"My baby," thought Samantha, looking down fondly at her

child's upturned face. "The one they told me I'd *never* have. . . ."

She remembered back to that night in the hospital. Her finest performance. It had been a terrible ordeal for her. After losing an earlier child by a miscarriage, she had been advised by her doctor to have an abortion when the new pregnancy occurred. But Samantha had wanted, more than anything else, to be a Mother and she was determined to try, no matter what the outcome. After long hours of pain and humiliation and in spite of terrible complications, Pandora was born.

It seemed as though she'd had the worst possible introduction to life and from there on in, things hadn't improved much. She'd grown up in an atmosphere of uncertainty and isolation. Her parents were unable to spend much time with her, so more often than not, she was obliged to sit alone in her room, immersed in some book or other. As it sometimes happens, it was this very lack of stability at home that made Pandora the strong, independent creature that she was. She seemed to have no capacity whatsoever for making friends. Perhaps schoolmates were discouraged by her air of independence, which could easily be misinterpreted as conceit, and besides, it was certainly true that she had little in common with other girls of the same age. Perhaps it was simply that she had grown up a little too quickly for her own good.

Samantha frowned.

"It's always the innocents who suffer," she thought to herself. "Now here I am, about to leave her again. . . . Or rather, she's leaving *me*."

"Mummy, you're *thinking* again! You're not to worry."

"Mmm?"

A portly middle-aged businessman paused by the door to examine the compartment, with the apparent intention of coming in. Pandora stuck her tongue out and blew a hearty raspberry in his direction. Outraged, he plodded away, looking for all the world like a furious pig.

"Pandora!" cried Samantha, putting her thoughts roughly aside. "That was very rude!"

"Sure. Got rid of him though, didn't it."

Samantha had to smile despite herself. "Little horror. Just see you mind your manners at your Aunt's house!"

"*Great-great* Aunt," corrected Pandora. "Golly, she must be really *old!*"

"Eighty-five, I think John said."

"Gosh. Do you think I'll ever live that long?"

The sound of slamming doors further down the train prevented Samantha from answering that rather awkward question. She jumped to her feet.

"Oh, my goodness, if I don't hurry along, I'll be going to Wales with you!" She gave Pandora a brief, fierce hug and hurried out of the compartment. Pandora followed her into the corridor and watched placidly as her Mother climbed down and slammed the door. A few late comers sprinted along the platform.

Pandora opened the window and leaned out.

"I'll write to you as soon as I get there," she cried.

Samantha reached up and kissed her. "Yes darling and I'll write straight back. . . . Oh here, look, we're making it sound like a prison stretch. It's a holiday. Have a good time!"

"Yes." Unconvincing.

"Oh, and don't forget. . . ."

"Mummy, please don't tell me to change at Swansea again!"

Samantha looked up at her daughter. She looked small and vulnerable, framed in the dusty window and somehow, in the grey gloom of morning, the station seemed a huge malignant place for such a child to be alone. A last few shreds of doubt wormed their way back into Samantha's heart.

"Darling, are you sure. . . ?"

Somewhere a whistle blew shrilly and Samantha's words were lost in the throaty roar of the train. It lurched and then began to move away. She followed a few steps, waving.

"See you after the holidays!" she cried.

"Bye Mummy! Love you!"

"You too, baby! Bye!"

And the train was gone, swaying into the distance. Samantha watched it dwindle, until the tiny, copper-haired figure waving at the window was too small to make out. She stood for a moment on the chilly platform and an abrupt sense of foreboding took her. The very air about her seemed charged with a grim alien coldness. She suddenly wanted, very much, to get out from under the grey roof of the station, into the morning sunshine.

Frowning, she turned away, startling a small flock of pigeons by her feet. They flapped upwards in alarm, the drumming of their wings sounding harsh and unreal in the silence.

Quickly, Samantha walked out of the station.

Chapter Two

Pandora chewed contemplatively on a cheese sandwich.

She had meant to save it for later, but she was bored already. The train rattled through flat, uninspiring countryside, broken only occasionally by a factory or industrial area. The sky was overcast and the colour of bruised flesh; it threatened rain.

Pandora sighed.

The train was only about half full and she still had the compartment to herself. She almost wished that she had allowed the businessman to enter. At least he would have been someone to talk to. But then, he had looked a boring sort anyway, the kind of man who would doubtlessly spend the entire journey engrossed in a newspaper. Why was it, she wondered, that she never encountered any of those handsome young men of the type that her Mother was constantly jumping into bed with, in her films. There was one in particular, a young man named Steve Asher, who had made his debut opposite Samantha in a film called "The Acid Summer." He was one of those golden-haired, suntanned types, who always looked out of place anywhere but on the beach. Lately, Pandora had taken to indulging in the most outrageous fantasies about him. . . . She was sure that if she ever met the man in person, she would be terribly disappointed.

She sighed. On the face of it, it seemed that for this summer at least, she would have to be content with her own company, and that of Aunt Rachel of course. She wondered vaguely what the old woman would be like. The only thing she knew for sure about Aunt Rachel was her age. She was eighty-five, twenty years older than Pandora's Grandmother!

Pandora had originally been destined to spend the summer holidays with her Gran, who lived in Southend. She hadn't minded that. For one thing, she loved her Gran's cottage and the gaudy town, with its amusement arcades, wax works, hot dog stalls . . . and the sea-shore, a good place for walking and being alone with her thoughts.

Besides, she was only too well aware of her parents' reasons for wanting to be alone. It was sad and complex and all too predictable. Due to the restrictions imposed upon them by their work, they were virtually strangers to each other, a husband and wife who met only occasionally and talked to each other even less.

The ridiculous thing was that they really did love each other; it was simply that they never had the time to notice. Pandora saw it all clearly, but said nothing. It was for them to iron out their differences and really, that was the idea behind this summer away from home. Samantha and John had cancelled all appointments for the next two months and intended to spend the time together, learning how to be a husband and wife again. Of course, they had never confided in Pandora about any of this but she was adept enough to figure it out for herself. Eager to help the idea along, she had herself suggested that she spend the summer with Gran. The whole visit had been duly arranged and things looked hopeful for the future. Pandora had visions of returning from Southend, to find her parents transformed into a couple of lovebirds. She suspected that she was being wildly optimistic, but then she had never been one for worrying unduly. The problem would resolve itself one way or another; she was at least confident of that.

Disaster struck only a week before the end of the school term. Grandmother had been taken ill and hospitalised; bronchitis, the doctors said. Grandfather, who was seventy-three and as deaf as a post, could hardly be expected to cope with a minor earthquake like Pandora.

The trip was off and that would have been the end of it, had Pandora not suggested Great-great Aunt Rachel.

She was a bit of an enigma, this one. The Ellises had first become aware of her existence about two years earlier, on one of the few mornings that they were all breakfasting together. Everyone was reading. John, the morning paper; Samantha, her latest script; Pandora, the homework she should have prepared the previous evening. She was also eating a bowl of corn flakes at the same time, not an easy task even for someone as practised as she.

A bundle of mail dropped through the letter box and fell with a slap in the hall. John grunted, wandered out, collected it, came back and resumed his seat. He sorted through the wad, disconsolately.

"Bill . . . bill . . . circular . . . bill . . . hello! This one looks interesting. Who do I know in Wales?"

If either Samantha or Pandora knew the answer to that question, they said nothing. John opened the envelope and took out a short, beautifully calligraphed letter. He read it with interest.

"Well, how about that?" he muttered when he had finished.

"How about what?" Samantha was interested enough to take her nose out of her manuscript for a few moments.

"This letter. . . ."

"Read it out," suggested Pandora.

"All right," John frowned. "The address at the top is 'Savannah' (I suppose that's the name of the house . . .), 'Bryn Myrddin. . . .'"

"Brin where?" cried Pandora.

"Bryn Myrddin. I think I'm pronouncing it right. . . . Carmarthen, South Wales. Anyway, this is the letter." He began to read.

Dear Mr. Ellis,

I felt I must write to congratulate you on your excellent romance, *Night of the Cicada*. As a young girl, I lived in Savannah, Georgia, and I feel that the way you have captured the colours and atmospheres of Southern America in the early nineteen hundreds is quite remarkable.

It may also interest you to know that we are related. I was your Grandfather's sister, which makes me, I believe, your Great Aunt. What a pleasant surprise to find that I have such a distinguished relative!

Please continue with your excellent writing and should you ever happen to be in this neck of the woods, do not hesitate to drop in and visit.

Yours sincerely,
(Miss) Rachel Ellis.

"Well, how about that?" murmured John. "A Great Aunt. . . ."

Pandora spoke through a mouthful of corn flakes.

"What does that make her to me then?"

"Er . . . Great-great Aunt, I suppose."

"Wow!" Pandora looked suitably awed. "Bet there aren't many kids with a *Great-great* Aunt, hey?"

"I expect not."

Samantha smiled. *"Night of the Cicada* . . . that rings a bell with me, somewhere. Wasn't it the one about the soldier of fortune, who fell in love with a rich widow. . . ?"

John winced visibly. "That's it," he admitted. "A truly degrading piece of literature it was, too; but, as I remember, I needed the money at the time."

"I rather liked it."

"Yes, well that doesn't surprise me one bit," muttered John, rather unkindly. "It was just up your street. A double helping of literary marzipan. At one time I even considered putting a sign on the cover. Danger! This book can cause tooth decay!"

Samantha shook her head.

"Well, if you hated it that much, why did you write the bloody thing?"

John picked up a handfull of bills from the table and waved them under Samantha's nose. "That's why!" he cried.

"Nonsense! The fact is that the book wasn't so bad at all. It was a damn sight better than that last thing you did . . . what was it called? Oh, yes, *Gothic Coffin.* I didn't understand one word of that!"

"Do you bloody well mind?" retorted John indignantly. "That book was little short of a masterpiece; why, did you read what the *Observer* said about it?"

"No, darling, what *did* the *Observer* say about it?"

John frowned. "Well . . . something like . . . I forget the

exact words they used, but it was something like . . . 'A riot of stark imagery, dark, intense and brutal.' Yes! Those *were* the exact words in fact; 'dark, intense and brutal'."

Samantha buttered a slice of toast.

"In other words, darling," she replied, "the *Observer* made about as much sense of it as I did. The sad fact is that, these days, any piece of work that defies understanding is immediately assumed to be a work of incomparable genius. It's the story of 'The Emperor's New Clothes' all over again. Nobody wants to admit that they're baffled by it. It's not their job to be baffled."

"Look, I hardly see what this has got to do with *Gothic Coffin.* . . ."

"It's got everything to do with it. As I recall, you were suffering with your ulcer all through writing the damned thing. You were so zonked on the Valium the doctor gave you, it's hardly any wonder none of it made sense."

"It did make sense!" protested John, loudly. "I admit that the storyline was a bit . . . disjointed . . . but that was purely symbolic of the . . . the hysteria of Twentieth-Century survival!"

"Balls!"

"Do you have to use that kind of language?"

"I'll use whichever language I bloody well like!"

They glared at each other across the table. Pandora, well schooled in the art of avoiding fights, saw her opportunity and took it.

"I liked *Gothic Coffin,*" she said soothingly.

They both stared at her.

"I didn't even know you'd read it darling," said Samantha.

"Of course! I've read all of Daddy's books. . . ."

John beamed triumphantly. "You see! Pandora has taste."

"But I liked *Night of the Cicada,* too."

"Oh." John returned to his breakfast. "Most people have children," he complained bitterly. "Me, I've got a diplomat. . . . Anyway, I must write back to Great Aunt Rachel. Amazing to think that she's still around. She must be one of the few 'American' Ellises left. . . . I notice her house is called 'Savannah.' Ten to one she's named it after her hometown; it's in Georgia, you know, where we Ellises originated from." He smiled. "Funny to think of a little bit of America marooned in the middle of all those Welsh rustics, isn't it?" He swallowed the last dregs of his coffee, got up and strolled over to the writing bureau. "Now, where did I leave the stationery set?" he mumbled.

Pandora smiled. "Writing back already then?"

"Yes . . . while it's still fresh in my mind. I'm planning a novel about Wales. . . ."

"You might know," interrupted Samantha, "that your father never takes the slightest interest in *anything*, without there being a book involved."

"What's that supposed to mean?" snapped John.

"Oh, nothing dear. Nothing at all."

Whatever John's reasons for writing that first letter, it marked the beginning of a steady correspondence that had lasted, to date, over two years. Great Aunt Rachel proved to be an inexhaustible source of interest; whether it was some cheerful anecdote, or memory culled from her youth, or whether she was commenting on current affairs, she wrote with a verve and sparkle that belied her venerable years. She had, it seemed, travelled to Wales from her native Georgia, in her early twenties, and had been so captivated by the country that she had never left it.

Right from the start, she took a deep interest in John and his family, especially Pandora. She would often ask for photographs and several times had suggested that the child might like to spend some time as her guest, in Carmarthen.

"It's such a wonderful place for children," she would say. "So full of interest. My house is set deep in the middle of a beautiful forest; it would make such a refreshing change for Pandora, from all that concrete and London grime."

So, when John, at Pandora's request, wrote to ask if it would indeed be possible for his daughter to stay at "Savannah," Aunt Rachel's reply was quick and affirmative. She would be delighted to have Pandora's company for the summer; the child would be no trouble at all.

John was quite happy with the arrangements, but Samantha was less easily reassured.

"After all," she argued, "it's not as if we've ever met the woman."

"Don't need to," replied John. "I've been writing to the old girl long enough to know all about her. She's the salt of the earth! Pandora will love her, you'll see."

"I hope so," muttered Samantha, frowning.

The train thundered into a tunnel.

Pandora was left staring at her own reflection in the window. She examined herself critically, grimacing at the snub nose and the huge blue eyes. She had always been dissatisfied with her own features. Why couldn't they be like Mother's, delicate and finely shaped? She poked her tongue out derisively and the freckled urchin face in the window followed suit.

She paused in her game. Her eyes widened in disbelief.

Now she was looking at the reflections of two faces. She could see quite clearly the image of a thin, pale, long-haired boy, peering over her shoulder, as though he was sitting on the seat immediately behind her. There was a bleak searching emptiness in the twin black pits that were his eyes.

Pandora sat there stunned for a moment, unable to tear her gaze from the boy's eyes. Then, with an effort, she spun around, only to discover that she was quite alone. The seat beside her was just as empty as it had been before. It was inconceivable that anyone could have entered the compartment from the corridor, nor escaped by that same route, in the brief few seconds it had taken her to turn around.

She was on the point of looking back to the window, when the train emerged once again into the daylight, leaving Pandora stunned and bewildered by the memory of that haunting, lonely face.

Somehow, she was unable to rid her mind of the image, all the rest of the journey.

Chapter Three

Carmarthen.

It was a station like many others.

Six hundred yards of grey concrete, dotted here and there with drab buildings; a book stall, a booking office, a dingy waiting room. At one time all three of its platforms had been in use, but now only the town side one was operative, the others stripped of their buildings.

It was well into the afternoon now, the sun touching low upon the horizon, reddening the wisps of cloud that clung there like discarded rags.

Pandora waited uncertainly upon the platform, clutching her small suitcase. She had missed her connection at Swansea and had been obliged to spend nearly two hours in a chilly waiting room. Glancing back, she saw a porter unloading her trunk onto a two-wheeled truck.

She frowned. She was to have been met here, or so Aunt Rachel had promised; but surely, nobody would have waited around the station an extra two hours? It certainly looked deserted. She dreaded the thought of trying to find her way to Aunt Rachel's house alone.

The porter hustled over with her trunk. He was a portly, red-faced man, with a huge grey walrus moustache.

"What's the matter, miss?" he inquired, in a rich Welsh accent. "A bit lost, you are looking."

Pandora couldn't help smiling at the man's jumbled English. "My name's Pandora . . . Pandora Ellis. . . ."

"Well, and very pretty you are, too, if I might make so bold! A bit young, though, to be travelling alone, I am thinking. . . ."

"I was supposed to be met here. Only I missed my train at Swansea and I don't know if my Aunt will have waited for me. . . . You haven't seen an old lady around the station have you?"

The porter shook his head. "I have not; though there *has* been a car waiting for some hours outside, I think."

"Pandora?" inquired a voice behind her.

She turned, surprised. Framed in the doorway of the ticket gate was a tall young man. He was swarthy and lean and the dying sun, throwing his figure into semi silhouette, gave him an inexplicable air of menace that was, in a strange way, very attractive. His eyes seemed to appraise Pandora coldly as he waited, frowning, his hands thrust deep into the pockets of his blue jeans. Pandora stared at him indecisively. She opened her mouth to speak but only a feeble stammer escaped.

"I . . . I . . . thought. . . ."

My name is Ewen. Rachel . . . that is, Miss Ellis, asked me to collect you. I've been waiting some time."

Pandora gazed up at him.

"*Heathcliffe*," she thought. "That should be his name. He's just how I've always imagined him."

"Is this your trunk?"

She nodded dumbly.

Ewen stepped forward and hefted the trunk up onto his powerful shoulders. "I'll put it into the station waggon," he said tonelessly and strolled out through the exit. Pandora stared after him in awe.

The porter smiled. "There you are, love! Problem solved . . . a holiday you are having, is it?"

She found her tongue at last.

"Uh . . . yes. A holiday."

"Enjoy yourself then. Good-bye now!"

"Bye. . . ."

The man wandered off down the platform, whistling cheerfully. Ewen re-emerged from the darkness of the exit and reached out his hand to take the suitcase. Pandora glanced down and saw that his hands were gnarled and knotted with thick dark veins. They looked very powerful, capable of causing great harm, should they be so inclined. The heavy suitcase seemed like a toy in his grasp.

"Through here," he muttered.

She followed him, handing her ticket to the collector as she went out.

The car sped along winding lanes.

Pandora sat hunched in the passenger seat, awaiting the opportunity to speak. She had never been at such a loss for words in her life. She glanced across at Ewen but his face was an expressionless mask, his eyes fixed intently on the road ahead. They had been driving for almost an hour and had not exchanged one word. Darkness was falling rapidly and Ewen had already switched on his headlights, their glare picking out the row of cats' eyes that stretched away into the night. Pandora studied Ewen carefully, wondering how she might start a conversation.

He was, she thought, somewhere in his late twenties and there was something in his swarthy complexion that hinted at foreign blood. His face was lean and his hard brown eyes were close set. His thick black hair hung over the collar of his denim shirt, and the dark stubble on his chin indicated that he was in bad need of a shave. The more Pandora looked at him, the more handsome he seemed to become. She thought it a shame that he wasn't smiling, because it would give him a softer, more agreeable look; and yet, there was something in his very sullenness that was exciting. Beside him, even the angelic Steve Asher seemed pale and unremarkable. The trouble was, he wasn't being over friendly. On the contrary, it was almost as though he was determined to make Pandora ill at ease by his indifference to her. Perhaps it was her lateness that had angered him.

She was itching to say something, for she hated having to stay silent at the best of times. She cleared her throat loudly, hoping to gain Ewen's attention, but his eyes never flickered from the road ahead. She fidgeted in her seat for a few moments and then decided to take the plunge.

"I'm sorry I was so late," she said. "I missed my connection."

No reply.

"Well, I hope you didn't mind waiting. . . ."

Again, no reply.

Pandora considered smacking Ewen across the ear, to see if that would cause any reaction, but she thought better of it. She decided instead, upon a straight question.

"Is it far to the house?"

"Few miles."

"A few?"

"'Nother half hour maybe." He had a strange, hard accent, hardly Welsh at all.

"Why . . . why didn't Aunt Rachel come to the station?"

He gave a mocking little laugh.

"Go out? *Her?* She never leaves the house!"

"Oh, why? Is she ill or something?"

"Something," replied Ewen tonelessly, his eyes staring into the path of the headlights.

The road was getting narrower by the minute and now a thick screen of forest flanked the road on either side, the trees looking like pale, spectoral giants in the brief flash of light. They seemed almost to be reaching out to each other, to form a thick roof overhead. Pandora was glad that she wasn't walking along this lonely stretch of road.

"It's certainly very wild here," she muttered.

No answer.

"This place we're going to. What's it called . . . Bryn something?"

"Bryn Myrrdin."

"Oh, yes. I wondered if it meant anything."

For the first time, Ewen turned in his seat and glanced at her. A curious smile played upon his lips. "Of course it means something," he replied. "It means Merlin's Hill."

"Merlin's Hill! Why's it called that?"

"Dunno."

Abruptly his gaze went back to the way ahead. The smile vanished, too.

Pandora frowned. It was obviously pointless to try and engage him in further conversation. She peered out of the window at the cloak of forest on her side. She was vaguely surprised at how dark it was; it was not yet eight o'clock but, here in the shadow of the trees, it might just as well be midnight. A grey mist was snaking low over the road and every now and then an isolated pocket of it drifted across the windscreen, momentarily obliterating all sight of the way ahead. Ewen didn't slow down for a moment. He guided the station waggon along the meandering lanes, like there was no tomorrow. Evidently, he knew where he was going.

Pandora sneaked another look at him.

"He's lovely," she thought to herself. "Like Heathcliffe. . . ."

She relaxed back in her seat and drifted off into a girlish fantasy, in which she and Ewen strolled laughing and talking through a corn field together. He was polite and charming and when she talked, he listened attentively, his head tilted to one side.

Pandora didn't realise it, but her long journey had tired her and the monotonous drone of the car engine was lulling her to sleep. Oddly, her fantasy continued on into the realms of her dreams, without even a break. But once there, it took a new, disturbing direction. The sunshine faded and the sky became grey and overcast. Flocks of great black crows flapped overhead, cawing loudly and a chill wind rustled through the stalks of corn, bending them earthwards. She turned to speak to Ewen and saw that he was slipping his shirt off and that he was staring at her with an intense hungry expression in his eyes. Despite the cold, his muscular arms and deep chest were dripping with thick beads of perspiration.

She stood rooted to the spot with fear; wanting to run, but unable to move so much as a muscle. Then Ewen was speaking to her, but in a strange unfamiliar language that she couldn't comprehend. He began to approach her, still talking and he was reaching down to unbuckle the thick leather belt around his waist. . . .

Suddenly, without warning, he reached out and grabbed her.

Chapter Four

She opened her eyes.

Ewen's hand was tugging insistently at her shoulder. "We're here," he said, and his voice seemed to come from a distance.

Pandora yawned, stretched, gazed around blinking owlishly. The car was now in a small, dimly-lit garage. Ewen got out of the car and went around to the back to collect the trunk. Pandora stumbled out, too, wiping the sleep from her eyes. Glancing at the luminous dial of her watch, she saw that she had only been sleeping for something like twenty minutes. Somehow, it seemed a lot longer. She stood there shivering slightly beside the car.

"This way," directed Ewen. He led the way out into the chill air of evening, the heavy trunk balanced easily on one shoulder, Pandora's suitcase clutched in his free hand.

Obviously, the garage was situated to the left side of the house and they emerged onto a ragged, overgrown lawn, surrounded on all sides by dense high walls of foliage. At one time, the garden had probably been quite magnificent; but now it was a veritable jungle of weeds and nettles and long clinging grass. From a distant gap in the hedgerow, a gravel drive led up to the front of the house, but this too was obscured in places by patches of moss.

Pandora and Ewen approached the house itself. It was a huge, sprawling mansion, three stories high and constructed of an ugly grey stone. Pandora knew very little about architecture, but guessed that it might be Georgian; she would have asked Ewen if she thought for one moment that she would receive an intelligent reply. She gazed up at the countless array of windows. All but a few of them were in darkness. The vast, imposing front door was situated beneath a stone porch, the flat roof of which was supported by two rows of Doric columns. It put Pandora more in mind of an ancient temple than a place for living in. She had had no idea that Aunt Rachel was as affluent as this. Silently, she followed Ewen up the ten marble steps to the door. Ewen set down the suitcase and fumbled in his pocket for a few moments. He produced a bunch of keys, set one of them in the lock and pushed the door open. They stepped through into a long hallway, the floor of which was set with brown and white tiles. From the roof above, hung a huge, but somewhat dusty, chandelier. It filled the hall with a harsh glare.

Ewen set down the trunk against a wall, with a slight grunt of relief. Then he pointed to a doorway on their left.

"Through there," he said simply. Without another word, he turned and walked on along the hallway, turning left at the end of it. Pandora heard his footsteps clumping up a staircase, out of her vision.

"Oh, dear," she muttered to herself. "I hope it's not all going to be like this. . . ." She was beginning to wish she'd never left home. Her visit had got off to a terrible start, if Ewen's attitude was anything to go by. He seemed to resent Pandora for some reason; surely he didn't blame her for being so late? After all, she hadn't missed her connection on purpose. She sighed and glanced at the door beside her. The worst was yet to come. She still had to meet her doddering old Great-great Aunt. She had decided it would be easier and more flattering, simply to refer to her as "Aunt Rachel."

"Better face the music, I suppose," she decided. She reached out for the door handle but thought better of it; instead, she tapped the door softly with her knuckles.

"Come in," suggested a woman's voice within.

Pandora tested the door. It creaked slowly open, revealing a spacious, rather old-fashioned sitting room. It seemed to be empty. Pandora walked in and closed the door after her. She gazed around slowly. The lights were low, but a huge log fire was blazing in the hearth, casting dancing reflections everywhere. Near to her was a small mahogany table, with four leather backed chairs. Further on, beside a large set of velvet drapes, which probably covered a french window, was an old leather sofa. Before the fire itself were two empty armchairs. No! Not both empty. Somebody was, in fact, sitting in the nearest of them, for Pandora could just discern the top of a head jutting up above the back of it.

"A . . . Aunt Rachel?" she inquired

"So, here you are at last," said an American voice. "I'd quite given you up. Come over here, where I can look at you."

Pandora had to suppress a gasp of surprise.

She had always understood that Aunt Rachel was eighty-five years old; but here she was, leaning back in an armchair, looking not a day over forty.

She had a thin, aristocratic face, that showed not one line of age upon it; her skin was soft and white as milk. She had a sharp proud nose and her large brown eyes were bright and full of mischief. Her hair, though tied up in a demure bun at the back, was a rich, natural honey colour; without a single streak of grey. Furthermore, she was wearing no makeup to achieve her youthful appearance.

Pandora's astonishment must have been evident because Aunt Rachel smiled, showing a set of even white teeth that were undoubtedly her own.

"Trying to catch flies?" she inquired.

Pandora closed her mouth hastily. "I'm sorry. . . ." she stammered. "It's just that . . . that is . . . you . . . I thought . . . you look so young!" she finished lamely.

Aunt Rachel smiled again. "Why, thank you," she said. "And I'm sure that with your company, I'll stay looking that way. It's our lovely Welsh air that does the trick, you know. Fountain of Youth." She motioned Pandora to the other chair. "Take the weight off those little legs. I declare, you must be near exhausted! Let's see about getting you a little supper. . . ."

She reached out her hand and took a small brass bell off a table beside her. She rang it briefly. It was surprisingly noisy, seeming to echo all through the house.

"Myfanwy will fix you something in no time," she said. Despite her years in Wales, she still possessed a rich, southern American twang to her voice, that was strangely soothing.

"How was the trip up from the station?"

"Oh . . . all right."

"Ewen keep you talking, huh?"

Pandora frowned. "Well, no . . . not really. He didn't say very much at all. I wondered if he was angry with me for being late."

Aunt Rachel chuckled. "No, I shouldn't think so. Fact is, that boy is no talker, never has been . . . a good man, though. It's just his way, that's all."

"Does he work here?"

"He's my gardener."

Instantly, that statement struck Pandora as odd. She remembered the state of the garden as she and Ewen had walked across it. It looked as though it hadn't seen a lawn mower in years.

The door opened and a stout, ruddy-faced woman bustled in, as though interrupted from some housework. Her red hair was tied back into a short, tight pigtail, emphasising the open, good nature of her twinkling blue eyes and broad smile. She was somewhere around middle age, dressed in a shapeless grey housecoat, which was rolled up at the sleeves, revealing two plump white arms. She was drying her hands on a small towel.

"Ah, Myfanwy," said Aunt Rachel. "This is the young lady I've been telling you about. Pandora, this is Myfanwy, my cook and housemaid. You'll be spending much of your time in her company while you're here. . . . Unfortunately, I suffer from an illness now and then. . . . It confines me to my room."

Myfanwy bowed slightly.

"Pleased to meet you, I am," she said.

"Hello." Pandora reached out and squeezed the woman's plump hand.

"Perhaps you can fix Pandora a little bite to eat," suggested Aunt Rachel. "She's had a long journey."

"Why, but of course! Some extra baking I have done. . . . I'll go see to it this minute."

She hurried out again, closing the door behind her.

Pandora leaned back in her chair and gazed around her. She was becoming more at ease by the minute. She studied her surroundings in more detail, noticing that the entire wall behind them was lined with bookshelves. There must have been something like a thousand volumes there. She let her gaze wander back to the fireplace and her attention was caught by a large painting that hung there. It was such a vivid picture that it was surprising she had not noticed it earlier. The painting showed a young girl, wearing a white nightdress and sitting on the edge of a small, alcove bed. Behind her, an open window revealed a full moon in the dark sky. The girl was probably no older than Pandora and she was very pretty, with long, straight blonde hair and a wistful little face. It was a wonderful picture of work. The girl's eyes seemed to burn from the canvas as though really alive; in fact, it was almost uncomfortable to return the gaze.

Aunt Rachel seemed to realise what Pandora was thinking.

"It *is* a fine picture, isn't it?" she sighed.

"It's *beautiful*. Who was the artist?"

"Ewen."

"Really? It's very good. . . . Does he paint a lot?"

"Very little, really. Perhaps I can persuade him to do one of you before you leave. . . ." A curious expression came into Aunt Rachel's eyes. For a moment she seemed to stare at something *beyond* Pandora. In fact, her stare was so intense that Pandora felt obliged to glance back, over the top of her own chair, expecting to see somebody come in through the doorway. But they were quite alone. She looked back to her Aunt whose fixed expression still seemed to indicate the presence of another.

Pandora felt decidedly uncomfortable.

"Who . . . who is the girl?" she asked, a little too loudly. She got out of her seat and walked nearer to the painting. Close up, the eyes seemed to positively implore the observer for help of some kind. Pandora was briefly reminded of the incident on the train; the mysterious reflection of a boy's face, that she'd seen so vividly for a couple of seconds. His eyes, too, had seemed to hold a similar message.

Aunt Rachel seemed to break free of her trance.

"Just some girl . . ." she muttered. "A relative of Ewen."

"I see. She's very pretty. . . ." Pandora broke off in bewilderment. In the bottom right hand corner of the painting, an indecipherable autograph had been sketched in with a fine brush. Underneath this was a date, presumably the date when the picture had been finished; but it was nineteen eighteen!

Surely that was impossible? Ewen was no more than twenty-five years old, thirty at the very outside. How then could he have painted the picture, before he was even born? Pandora frowned. She glanced back at Aunt Rachel who seemed not to have noticed a thing. A thought occurred to her. Aunt Rachel was eighty-five, but looked only forty. . . . Perhaps then, Ewen was much older than he looked. . . . She did some quick mental arithmetic and almost instantly discarded the idea. He couldn't possibly be that old! Thoughtfully, she went back to her seat. Perhaps the date on the painting meant nothing; perhaps it was a joke. Still, it was puzzling. . . .

"And what do you think of our lovely country?" inquired Aunt Rachel.

"Oh . . . well, I've not seen any of it, yet. I fell asleep in the car."

"Perhaps tomorrow you might like to take a stroll in the forest; it's very near, almost on our doorstep and quite the loveliest place. I only wish I could get out like I used to . . . the time I used to spend there!"

"Yes; it sounds nice." Pandora found her eyes constantly straying back to the young girl's portrait. She made a conscious effort to mentally change the subject.

"What a lot of books you have, Aunt Rachel!"

"Oh, yes. I do a lot of reading, Pandora, though I must confess that most of these books were here when I moved into the house; they were bequeathed to me by my Uncle. Over in the corner there, I have several of your Father's novels. He's a fine writer."

"Yes, I think so, too."

"Was it his idea to call you Pandora?"

"No, it was Mummy's. She's always been interested in mythology. Do you know the story of Pandora's Box?"

Aunt Rachel frowned. "I seem to remember it from my schooldays. Wasn't it the one where a young lady was presented with a pretty little casket, then told that on no account must she open it?"

"That's right! Of course, curiosity got the better of her and she opened it up and out flew a great swarm of troubles and illnesses, that have plagued the world ever since."

"Hmm. Not the most flattering name in the world, then. . . ."

Pandora smiled. "Mummy told me once that she didn't even know why she'd picked that name. She just woke up one morning and there it was in her head. Try as she might, she couldn't seem to shake it out. . . . Anyway, I guess I kind've lived up to it as a toddler, always poking my nose into things and causing terrible accidents."

"Accidents?"

"Oh, nothing really bad of course! Knocking things over mostly, general clumsiness, you know. Mind you, I nearly set fire to the house once, I remember! For some reason I removed a screen from the fireplace and a cinder fell onto the carpet. Luckily, my Father smelled burning before the fire got too much of a hold. . . . Isn't it funny how a person's name seems to affect how they turn out? I mean, if my name was Jane or Mildred, I'd most probably be a completely different person."

"And do you like yourself, the way you are?"

Pandora shrugged. "I suppose so."

The door opened and Myfanwy came in with a tray of food and drink. She took it over to the small mahogany table and set it down. "There, now," she said. "Some homemade bread I have brought and some cheese; and a big slice of sponge cake. If you are wanting more, just sing out!" She motioned to Pandora who slipped out of the armchair and seated herself at the table. She needed no second bidding to start. The long journey had given her a keen appetite. She took a mouthful of the thickly buttered wholemeal bread. It was delicious and she said so. Myfanwy beamed with obvious pleasure and went back about her business. Pandora ate rapidly, finishing up every last crumb. Aunt Rachel watched her quietly.

"There's nothing wrong with your appetite," she observed as Pandora pushed her empty plate aside and got up from the table.

"Must be the country air. I'm not usually such a pig!" She patted her stomach happily. "Myfanwy's a wonderful cook. I must try and get her recipe for bread before I leave."

"Myfanwy's very talented in the kitchen all right; which is pretty lucky. It's quite a way into the nearest village, Brechfa. That's where Myfanwy lives, but she stays here through the week and bikes home on Friday night; takes her a good couple of hours to get home! Sunday evening she gets on back here, just

in time to make supper. Of course, Ewen drives over to the village once or twice a week for supplies and things; he'll post letters for you when you want to write to your Mother and, of
course, if there's anything special you need you only have to ask.
I expect it will make a great change for you from London. It's
really very quiet here."

"You don't go out yourself much?"

"No, never!" Aunt Rachel seemed almost shocked at the idea.
"My . . . illness you see. . . ."

"Oh, but you look so well!"

"It's a nervous complaint. Affects my legs . . . sometimes I
can't even stand, let alone walk."

"What a shame."

"Yes, well let's not dwell on my misfortunes. . . . Perhaps
you'd like to see your room now, settle all your things in. I'll get
Ewen to take your baggage up if you like."

"Yes . . . all right." Pandora got the impression that she wasn't
actually being given a choice in the matter. But anyway, she *was*
fairly tired.

She waited patiently as her Aunt reached out and rang the
small brass bell.

Ewen led the way up the big staircase, the trunk balanced
rather precariously on his right shoulder. Pandora and Myfanwy
followed close behind.

The staircase itself was a thing of monumental beauty, constructed from glossy dark wood, with a bannister rail that was
intricately carved into the form of gargoyles' faces, each one
more unspeakably deformed than its predecessor. The rail was
so high that Pandora could just see over it when she stood on
tiptoe.

"It's such a *big* house," gasped Pandora.

"Oh, yes!" replied Myfanwy. "It is big, right enough. Though
all of it we don't use . . . the top floor is all boarded up. Just the
three of us here, it was silly to keep it going. So much cleaning
there was!"

"Yes, I suppose there must have been."

Pandora turned her attention to the row of faded portraits that
adorned the wall on her right side. There were many thin men
with gaunt, hawk faces and fat men with contented vole-like

faces and young ladies in outrageous feathered hats and, now
and then, the occasional ruddy-cheeked child cuddling a dog.

"Who are all those people?"

Myfanwy shrugged. "I only know one or two of them . . . but
they have all lived here, at one time or another. A very *old* place
it is!" She paused before a portrait of a stocky, middle-aged man
with thick red curly hair. "This one's the old master," she said.
"Miss Rachel's Uncle. A great scholar he was, they say."

Pandora studied the man's brooding features; the small piggy
eyes, almost hidden beneath clumps of red eyebrow; the soft
flabby cheeks; the huge bulbous nose; the strange, slightly dis-
concerting smile. It was not a pleasant face at all and yet, oddly
enough, it reminded her in some way of Aunt Rachel. Myfanwy
must have guessed her thoughts, because she said, "Yes! A likeness there is, I've always thought that! Subtle, though. I've never
yet worked out just what it is. Something. . . ."

They continued on their way, up onto the first floor landing.
Ewen stood waiting by a door at the head of the stairs. Myfanwy
motioned him to go in and he did so, switching on an electric
light as he passed.

"You'll like this room," said Myfanwy, as they entered. "Might
have been made for you; mind, it's been a good few years since
anyone slept here. But all it needed was a good airing and as
good as new it is!"

It was indeed a lovely little room. For some reason it struck
Pandora as being vaguely familiar. She looked slowly around,
noting the wardrobe, the writing desk and the little alcove bed
that could be partitioned off from the rest of the room, by means
of a white muslin curtain. It was, by its very size and character,
a child's room. To the left a dressing table was already set out
with a few girlish effects, a hairbrush and comb and a small,
round mirror. The window above the bed was open and looked
out onto the garden. Out in the night the grasshoppers were
singing.

"It's lovely," said Pandora enthusiastically. "Really lovely!"

Ewen set down the trunk beside the bed. He stood for a moment, his hands in his pockets, his face expressionless. He looked
a little clumsy and uncomfortable in the tiny room. Then,
abruptly, without a word he turned and, pushing past the others,

went out onto the landing and down the stairs. Pandora gazed after him thoughtfully.

"You mustn't mind him now," cautioned Myfanwy. "An odd sort, he is, but through no fault of his own."

"How . . . how old is he?"

"Not sure. About twenty-five, I think. . . . Why?"

"Oh, I just wondered. He's certainly a wonderful painter. . . ."

"A what?" Myfanwy seemed rather surprised.

"Well, yes . . . that picture in the sitting room. The one of the young girl."

"Oh, that. Yes." Myfanwy set Pandora's suitcase down on the bed. "Shall we unpack your things, then?" she suggested.

But Pandora didn't hear her. She had just that second realised why the room had seemed familiar to her at first glance. The conversation had served to trigger her mind; and now, it was almost as though she could see Ewen's painting again, in every tiny detail.

"This is the room!" she cried. "It's the *same room!* I'm positive."

"We can start putting your dresses in the wardrobe. . . ."

"The one in the painting, Myfanwy! I recognise it! This is the same room. That's the same bed that the little girl is sitting on."

Myfanwy shrugged. "Oh, I shouldn't think so. . . ."

"But it is!" Pandora looked at her companion searchingly. "Anyone can see that. That must mean that the little girl, the one in the picture, has stayed here before!"

Myfanwy opened the wardrobe and glanced inside.

"Well, that I wouldn't know. I have not always worked here, you see. . . . Perhaps a long time ago she might have stayed here."

"Nineteen eighteen," murmured Pandora.

"What?"

"Oh, nothing. Just thinking out loud; but look, Myfanwy, it couldn't have been done that long ago, could it? Not if Ewen was the artist!"

They stood in silence for a few moments, staring at each other. Myfanwy seemed to be searching for a way to answer the question. She looked rather worried. At last she simply said:

"Shall we unpack, then?"

Pandora nodded. "Yes," she replied. "All right."
They went about the task in silence.

Pandora lay in bed, listening to the sounds of the old house as
it creaked and murmured beneath the caress of the night winds.
Here, an old oak beam, bent and infirm, eased its backbone with
a groan of discomfort; there, a prying tendril of air prised loose a
roof tile and sent it clattering earthwards. In between the occasional noises, the house rippled its millions of nerve endings and
screamed coffee warm silence into the deserted upper rooms.

It was late and Pandora was tired but, somehow, sleep eluded
her. She kept thinking of the beautiful painting and its mysterious date. Of course, it had to be a joke or a mistake or . . . something. Her own reason should have served to convince her of
that. But each time she set her thoughts aside, they crept insistently back across the pillow and into her head, where they
wriggled like a swarm of troublesome insects. And besides, there
was *something* going on in this house, a secret, a mystery, an intrigue, of that she was fairly sure. Ever since she was very
young, she had possessed an uncanny ability to sniff out secrets;
perhaps it stemmed from years of having to discover for herself
the latest source of friction between her warring parents. Savannah fairly reeked of a secret, perhaps one that was as old as the
house itself.

Pandora sighed. It was a warm night and the air in the little
room was stale. She pushed aside her blankets, sat up and drew
back the curtains of the little window. Then she opened it wide
and leaned out, breathing the night air deep into her lungs. It
tasted clean and delicious with the fragrance of flowers. She
gazed down at the tangled garden. It looked rather forbidding in
the moonlight, a perfumed jungle of shrubs and grasses.

Somewhere, a solitary bird trilled a delicate song. Pandora
frowned. For the first time since the farewell at Paddington Station, she was really missing her home. It was hardly the company of her parents that she yearned for. After all, she rarely saw
that much of them. But she was thinking of her own bedroom,
complete with its shelves of books, the painting easel and a
ready supply of canvases. That place was her refuge against the
rest of the world, a place where she didn't have to worry about
making friends or keeping herself tidy. This room was nice

enough, of course, but as yet, it was unfamiliar to her. She thought back to Ewen's painting again and wondered vaguely what had happened to the little girl. If the date on the picture was correct, then she would have grown up and turned into a grey-haired old lady by now. And yet she was supposed to be a relative of Ewen. . . . Most likely the date inscribed was more like nineteen *sixty*-three and she had simply misread it.

A sudden movement out amongst the bushes made Pandora jump. She stiffened slightly and peered intently into the night; somewhere out in the blackness she'd glimpsed a brief flash of white moonlight reflecting on a moving shape. She listened for a few moments, but there was only silence, total and unreal. Even the bird had ceased his lonely cries.

Perhaps then it had been her imagination . . . but no! There again was a movement. Not a rustle of vegetation as might have been expected, but a smooth, silent journey beneath the gaze of the moon.

Pandora stared down in awe.

The boy emerged from a clump of bushes and began to make his way across the lawn. He was quite naked and his bare flesh looked deathly white against the velvet backdrop of the garden. He moved rapidly across the grass in a swift, gliding run. Pandora could see quite plainly that his feet never once touched the ground.

He was about halfway across the lawn when his head turned to stare blindly in Pandora's direction, as though he was aware of her small figure framed in the upstairs window. For an instant his frightened eyes bored relentlessly into hers, pleading, invoking.

It was the same boy. The one she had seen on the train. As she watched helplessly, he seemed to float right through the trunk of a gnarled oak tree and vanished from her sight, as though he had been swallowed whole by the greedy darkness.

Only then did the night bird resume his interrupted song.

Chapter Five

A shaft of sunlight found its way through a gap in the curtains and onto Pandora's face. She awoke blinking, and gazed around, surprised by her unfamiliar surroundings, until she remembered where she was.

She lay still for a few moments, staring up at the ceiling. She could tell that it was a fine morning, without even moving. Through the open window wafted a pleasing mixture composed of equal quantities of warmth and birdsong. From somewhere below came the sounds of Myfanwy humming a tune as she went about her duties and from the garden came a steady clumping sound as though someone was chopping wood.

It was only then that Pandora recalled what she had seen the previous night. She was quite positive that it had been a ghost and oddly, the thought didn't frighten her. She would have liked to tell someone about it, but who? Who was there in this big, gloomy house that she felt she could trust? Certainly not Ewen. Definitely not Myfanwy, who had proved to be so evasive the night before. That only left young-old Aunt Rachel. She had given Pandora no grounds to distrust her and yet, wasn't there something about her that didn't sit easy on the mind? No, the whole incident was best kept to herself, at least for the time being. Maybe the boy would visit her again, as he had on the train. Perhaps he himself had a secret to confide and had chosen Pandora as his ally.

She yawned, stretched, and climbed lightly out of bed. She peeked through the curtains. Sure enough, there was Ewen at the far end of the garden, standing beside a large stack of logs and hacking into them with an axe. He was stripped to the waist and the sweat glistened on his tanned skin. He worked steadily, almost mechanically, never pausing to wipe away the beads of perspiration that trickled down his forehead. Pandora found herself fascinated by Ewen's powerful body, the way that his muscles rippled beneath his flesh as he worked. She noticed the dark scowl on his face. It was almost as though he hated the inanimate objects that bore the brunt of his attack. Pandora watched him for some moments before turning away and dressing hurriedly in jeans and T-shirt and battered old tennis shoes. Then she picked up her washbag and towel and went out to the bathroom which was the next door along from hers. She noticed that the door to the third room, which Myfanwy had told her was Aunt Rachel's, was still shut.

As Pandora brushed her teeth, she was surprised to hear a brief clumping noise from the floor above. She frowned. Myfanwy had said that it was all boarded up and unused. She listened again but there was no further sound.

She strolled back to her room and dumped her things, then made her way downstairs. The sitting room was empty. "Hello" she called. "Anyone about?"

"Through here," replied Myfanwy's voice. "In the kitchen."

Pandora followed the sound of the voice, through what looked like a large dining room, into a spacious and very modern kitchen. Myfanwy was busy at the stove, cooking bacon and eggs.

"Just doing your breakfast," she called over her shoulder.

"Smashing!" Pandora sat down at a small table. "But how did you know I was up?"

"Heard you moving about, I did! There is not much that I miss, you know! Miss Ellis always says that I have ears like vacuum cleaners . . . they pick up all the dirt!" She chuckled happily as she heaped the food onto a plate. "Did you sleep all right?"

"Fine, thanks."

"Good. And what are you planning to do with yourself today?"

"I'm not really sure. Just have a wander about, I should think. Didn't Aunt Rachel say something about a forest. . . ?"

"Yes, just at the bottom of the road," agreed Myfanwy, setting down Pandora's breakfast. "A lovely place it is, too . . . but mind you don't get lost now! Very deep, it is, in parts."

"I won't. I've got a good sense of direction." Pandora ate hungrily. "Think I'll take my sketchbook along with me . . . make a day of it."

"A little lunch I could pack for you, if you like."

"Well . . . if it would be no trouble. . . ."

"Not a bit of it! A pleasure!" She turned away and busied herself taking various things out of the large refrigerator.

"It's a lovely kitchen," observed Pandora.

Myfanwy beamed. "Wonderful, it is . . . thanks to Miss Ellis, of course. Paid for everything. Had men up from the city to see to it. Had everything modernised. 'Never mind the cost!' she said. 'My cook shall have the best!' You should have seen the black old boiler that was here when I moved in-. . . . How the people before me managed, I'll never know. . . ."

"Aunt Rachel not up yet?"

"No. I often don't see her at all until the evening. Her legs, you know. . . ."

"Yes, she told me; only she must be up and about, because I heard her moving around on the top floor."

Myfanwy turned around suddenly, a strange expression on her usually placid face. She had a look that was hard to define; its roots lay somewhere between surprise and fear. All the colour had drained from her face. It was a sudden and startling transformation.

"No!" she snapped. "No, you're wrong! It's all closed up, that floor. You couldn't have heard anyone."

"But I did, Myfanwy." Pandora stared back coolly. "Someone was walking about. I wouldn't lie to you."

Myfanwy seemed to get a hold on herself. She turned away.

"I'm not saying you were lying, miss."

"What, then?"

"Mistaken, that's all. The old beams, you see . . . half falling apart, they are. Wouldn't surprise me if they fell in one day, nei-

ther, and us all lying here in our beds." Pandora watched Myfanwy's hands as she cut a slice of cheese. The knife blade was
shaking visibly.

"I . . . suppose you're right," she said thoughtfully. "Now I
think of it, it wasn't really like anyone walking. Just a couple of
thumps."

"Yes, that would be the beams, you see. The beams. . . ."

Pandora got the distinct impression that Myfanwy was trying
to reassure herself more than anyone else. There followed a long,
uncomfortable silence broken only by the distant thud! thud!
thud! of Ewen's axe out in the garden. Pandora finished off the
remnants of her breakfast thoughtfully, while Myfanwy packed
sandwiches into a plastic lunch box.

After a few minutes Pandora excused herself and made her
way back upstairs, intending to collect her sketchbook. But
something made her pause before going into her room. She
glanced down the landing at Aunt Rachel's door, still tight shut
against the world.

"What is it that Myfanwy's afraid of?" she wondered.

Hesitantly, she walked towards it and stood listening for a moment. Not a sound came from within. She reached out and
tapped softly with her knuckles. No reply. She tried again, a little harder this time. Still, no reply. She shrugged, went back to
her own room and, finding her sketch pad and pencils, she
slipped them into a canvas shoulder bag.

As she came out again she heard, quite distinctly, four rapid
bangs from the ceiling above her head. She paused to listen for a
moment.

Another thud, then a rustling, slithering sound, as though
something was being dragged or pushed across the floor. Then a
flurry of little taps and clatters. Pandora frowned. Whatever was
making those noises, it certainly couldn't be attributed to worn-
out beams. Resolutely, she turned and strode to the end of the
hall. A dusty, rickety staircase led upwards to the left but, halfway along it, a screen of jagged boxwood had been nailed across,
higgledy-piggledy, to bar the way. Pandora was not convinced.
She stepped cautiously onto the first step and it creaked protest-
ingly beneath her weight, but she continued on her way. Glancing down, she noticed that a path had been kept free of dust
along the middle of the stairs, as though someone had been

using it regularly. She reached the wooden screen and examined it carefully. It didn't take her a moment to discern that a large, vertical slat was nailed only at the top and easily hinged open, so that a grown person might slip through the gap; it swung quietly back at Pandora's touch and she peered into the blackness beyond.

A blast of icy air clawed at her face, actually making her lean back for a moment. The wind brought with it a powerful, unpleasant odour, a stale, mouldering, mummy-bandage smell. Pandora wrinkled up her nose in repugnance. Away in darkness, she thought she could hear a brief, shuffling sound.

"Aunt Rachel?" she called softly. "Are you in there?"

Her voice seemed to dance, hollow and alien, along unseen corridors. The last echoes died.

Silence.

Pandora shook her head. She'd never been too frightened of the dark, but somehow she didn't much fancy blundering in there without a light. Anyway, if Aunt Rachel was hiding away behind the screen, it was obvious that she had her own reasons for not being interrupted. Pandora let the wood swing back, cutting off the smell of mildew and decay. Then she turned and went back down the stairs, deep in thought.

The forest was beautiful.

Pandora wandered slowly along a barely defined track, marvelling at the soft, springy touch of the earth beneath her sneakers. She gazed up and about at the multitude of gnarled treetrunks that everywhere sprang upwards to support a canopy of whispering foliage. Here and there, an occasional shaft of sunlight pierced the gloom and dappled the ground, giving it the appearance of being at the bottom of an ever-restless ocean. It was cool, too, and fragrant with primroses and wild daffodils that grew here and there in scattered explosions of colour, on either side of the track.

Pandora paused to glance at her watch and was surprised to find that she had been walking for several hours. It had seemed like no more than a few minutes. Her lunch lay, as yet untouched, in the canvas shoulder bag, along with her sketchbook and pencils. She had intended to do some drawing, but every time her eye fell on a worthy subject, something of greater interest distracted her. She felt strangely exhilarated by her walk; there was a vibrant, tingling glow all through her body. She stood absolutely still for a moment, sensing her own smallness beneath the great, threatening trees. She turned slowly around in a full circle. As far as she could see, the vegetation was equally as thick on all sides. It would have been possible to walk for hour after hour, in any direction, and never see another soul.

She moved on again, her head filled to bursting with the songs of a myriad of birds. In amongst the trees, their chirruping and trilling was as piercing as the chiming of countless little bells.

Now the ground began to slope away abruptly and she half walked, half ran down the incline, laughing wildly at her own inability to stop. At the bottom of the curve, a shallow but furious stream crossed her path, gurgling and splashing. It was too wide to leap across but somebody had thoughtfully provided a series of flat, grey stepping stones. Without hesitation, Pandora embarked on a perilous crossing, her arms outflung like a tightrope walker. She imagined that she was crossing Niagara Falls while a crowd of anxious admirers looked on in suspense. Icy water snatched at her ankles and halfway across, she squatted down to stare into the glittering shallows. A couple of small, silvery fish seemed to hover just beneath the surface, unaffected by the powerful current. Pandora stretched out her fingers to them and they sped nervously away from her. She straightened up, chuckling and hop-skip-jumped her way to the far shore. The path led upwards again and she accepted its invitation, plunging recklessly through a thick screen of bushes. She found herself in a place that was, if anything, darker than the woods that she had already explored. Here, the trees grew in incredible contortions, often taking on the appearance of men's faces; long bulbous noses; baggy, close-set eyes; twisted wizened mouths. One even had a bony head, topped by thick layers of grey fungus, that hung down on either side like unkempt sideboards. The trees seemed to grow even thicker here, too, sometimes touching each other. Pandora's progress became more and more erratic as she was obliged to stoop beneath or even bypass completely, a tangle of groping branches.

Just as she was considering turning back in search of another path, she emerged into a large clearing, where the trees were very widely spaced indeed. This was obviously a natural phenomenon, because there were no stumps in sight. She took a few steps forward into the clearing, then paused, vaguely aware that something was wrong. She glanced quickly about but everything seemed to be in order. Even so, a distinct "alien" feeling stuck firmly with her.

She suddenly realised what was different.

It was the birds. They had stopped singing.

Only seconds before, there had been a beautiful cacophony of sound. Now there was only silence. Pandora thought of the ghost boy she'd seen the previous night and the way that a single night bird had fallen silent when he appeared. Then, in the comparative safety of the house, she hadn't been afraid. Here, alone and vulnerable in the huge, gloomy forest, she wasn't anything like as comfortable. She licked her lips nervously, glancing this way and that. A couple of times she thought she detected a slight movement, but on closer examination it proved to be only the sunlight dancing upon some long grass.

"Silly!" she admonished herself fiercely. "It's your imagination, that's all!"

"Well," countered a second voice within her head. "What about the boy in the garden? I suppose that was imagination, too. . . ."

Angry with herself for being such a faintheart, she moved resolutely forward across the clearing, whistling tunelessly to herself. The strange atmosphere stayed with her, though, as if the very air itself had been charged with an inexplicable taste of menace. Her attention was now drawn to a huge, misshapen oak tree in the very centre of the clearing. It was completely devoid of leaves and the trunk seemed to soar straight upwards without the presence of a single branch, until its summit was lost amongst the shadows of the neighboring foliage. The roots of the tree were very spectacular; outflung like the groping tentacles of some huge octopus, they were undermined by a large, burrow-like opening, several feet in diameter. Pandora paused and bent to stare down into the hole. She could dimly make out a deep, smooth tunnel leading downwards for a few yards and then there was only darkness. She wondered what kind of animal could have made such an opening in the hard earth.

The bark of the tree itself was choked with a thick growth of brightly coloured ivy near its base. Pandora decided that she would like to press one of the leaves in her sketchbook, so she reached out to tear a handful of ivy away from the wood. It was extraordinarily tenacious and she had to exert considerable effort to pull it down. However, the removal of the leaves revealed something far more interesting beneath; namely, a small oblong plate of black corroded metal, fixed firmly to the trunk. It had obviously been placed there many years before, because several layers of bark had intruded over the edge of the plate, sinking the metal several inches into the face of the tree. Intrigued, Pandora ripped more tendrils of ivy away. She peered at the plate closely, thinking that she could discern a slight pattern beneath the corrosion, something made up of several wavy lines. She rubbed at the metal with her fingers, but to little effect.

"That's no good . . ." she muttered aloud. "Need something . . . sharp. . . ."

She remembered the lunch that Myfanwy had packed for her and reaching into her shoulder bag, she took out the paper parcel and dumped it unceremoniously onto the grass. Sure enough there was the rattle of knife against fork. Grinning, she unwrapped the parcel, extracted the knife and set to the task with vigour, scraping away at the ancient metal with the flat of the blade.

Sure enough, the relief pattern began to show through, silver against the dull black. But it was more than just a pattern! Pandora could now recognise letters, words. She worked diligently until she could read the whole thing. There were just two lines of writing in all and it was obviously Welsh. It read:

Pan fyrd Jeruen Myrdyn
Ve fyrd Tre Kervyrdyn.

Pandora thought she recognised one of the words as meaning "Merlin" even though it seemed to be spelt differently from "Bryn Myrrdin"; "Merlin's Hill." She wanted to know what the rest of the little couplet meant. She decided to note the words down in her sketchbook, so that she could ask Myfanwy about it later. She did just that, even trying to copy the erratic style of lettering that formed the original. That done, she put the incident out of her mind and, leaning back against the tree, she gave Myfanwy's packed lunch the attention it so rightly deserved.

Even now, she did not feel completely at ease in the clearing.

The silence was still oppressive and it was rather cold, although the sun was blazing up above the tree line. She kept glancing about nervously as though expecting at any moment to see a mysterious figure, flitting spectre-like amongst the trees. She looked at her watch. Twenty past four.

"I suppose I ought to make a move," she muttered aloud. She reached out a hand for the shoulder bag, which lay by her side, and saw, to her surprise, that a large olive-green lizard had emerged from the dark burrow beneath the tree roots and was watching her intently with its malignant red eyes. With a sharp intake of breath, Pandora snatched back her hand and sat regarding the sleek, wrinkled creature in horrified fascination. It was slightly over a foot long, from nose to tail, and its ancient face was oddly intelligent. It seemed to be studying her, a weird smile on its long, curving mouth, from which a black, forked tongue slid smoothly in and out.

"Shoo!" she cried. "Go away!"

The thing didn't flinch for an instant, just lay there in the dust, watching calmly.

"I said Shoo!" Pandora lashed out with her foot, raining a shower of dirt over the lizard. With a sudden squeak, it jerked around and skittered back down the hole, out of sight. Pandora snatched up her bag and jumped to her feet, her heart hammering in her breast. The beast's abrupt action had startled her.

"Horrid thing!" she exclaimed. She certainly didn't feel like going any further now. Without hesitation she hurried back in the direction she had come from. Once she thought she detected a rustling noise amongst the trees to her left and it took all her willpower to keep from running. It was simply her imagination getting the better of her, that was all. It had been the lizard's sudden movement that had unnerved her, that and the terrible silence.

Amazingly, as she broke through the undergrowth that bordered the clearing, the bird song was resumed as suddenly as if a tape recording had been switched on. The sound of it was reassuring to say the very least; but it was puzzling that it couldn't be heard at all from the clearing. "The leaves must form a kind of soundproof barrier," decided Pandora.

She strolled back along the path in the vague direction of "Savannah." After a few minutes the ground began to veer downwards towards the stream and the vegetation grew sparser, letting the sun extend its gentle fingers downwards to warm the earth. Halfway down the slope Pandora paused.

Seated on the near bank of the stream, his back to her, was a boy. He was stripped to the waist and his long, black hair hung thick over his shoulders. He was fishing with a homemade rod and obviously had not heard Pandora's approach because of the gurgling water. From the back, he resembled the wandering ghost boy that she had seen in Aunt Rachel's garden; and yet, here in the warm afternoon sunshine, he seemed real enough, casting a fairly substantial shadow on the grass. Pandora moved forward cautiously, unsure of what to do. Perhaps she should creep back without disturbing him, find another place to cross the stream . . . but if she did that, she would never know if he was the same boy or not. And supposing he was? What would she do? What would she say? "Worry about that if and when it happens," she thought. Against her better judgment, she moved inexorably nearer, half expecting the seated figure to disappear in a flash of light. Soon she was standing a mere three feet behind him.

She stood waiting uncertainly for a moment, wishing he would turn around of his own accord. But he was too intent upon watching his improvised cork float dancing on the water.

"Oh, well," thought Pandora. "Here goes, then. . . ."

She drew herself up to her full height and cleared her throat. "Hello," she said at last.

Chapter Six

The boy jumped ever so slightly.

He turned slowly around and regarded Pandora with a look akin to contempt. He was not the ghost boy at all. He was someone even more perplexing. Pandora found herself looking at Ewen, or rather, she found herself looking at a boy who was Ewen's youthful equivalent. He possessed the same dark, smouldering eyes as the gardener, the same swarthy face and lean cheeks. All that was missing was the thick chin stubble which, as yet, he was obviously too young to cultivate. Lord, but what a place of mysteries Bryn Myrrdin was! It seemed to Pandora that she had only been there ten minutes and already she had encountered more weird happenings than she had in her twelve years of existence. It was almost as though she had left home and entered a new world of intrigue that dictated its own laws.

She realised that the boy was still watching her with a puzzled expression on his face. She smiled in what she hoped was a reassuring manner.

"Where did you appear from?" demanded the boy.

"The forest. I'm sorry for creeping up on you. I thought you were someone else. . . ."

"There's no one else here."

"No. I can see that now." Pandora moved forward and sat herself boldly beside him at the water's edge. "What are you doing?" she inquired good-naturedly.

"What does it look like?" he replied.

"Well . . . you know what I mean. . . . Have you caught anything?"

He returned his gaze to the bobbing cork. "Not yet . . . only been here a few minutes, haven't I!"

"Oh. Well, I shouldn't think there are many fish here. It's not deep enough, is it?"

He shook his head. "Shows how much you *know!* Fish here quite often, I do. There's dace in here. . . . Dace like water to be shallow and fast. Caught *hundreds* of dace here, haven't I!"

Pandora smiled. "I suppose you're right," she admitted. "I don't know anything about fishing. . . . Why, I've never even *been* fishing, not in my whole life!"

"Of course not. You're a *girl.*" He pronounced the word in the same way that he might say "Frog" or "Snail."

Pandora shrugged, nodded, admitting the hopelessness of her sex. "It's a drag, being a girl," she sighed. "I hate it. I'd love to play football, go fishing. . . ." She thought suddenly of her father on a grey, rainy Sunday in the distant past, all dressed up in rainproof mac and Wellington boots. She'd begged him to take her then, but he'd just hummed and haahed about it being "unsuitable for a young lady," or some such rubbish. That very evening, she'd gone up to her bedroom, selected a suitably expensive doll and danced up and down on it, until it was so much shattered plastic. In those times, she had wanted to be a boy more than anything in the world. It was plain to her that they had so much more going for them, that it was the ragged little males with their scabby knees and half crown catapults who would inherit the earth. These days she had learned to live with her role more easily, but it still hurt sometimes to be reminded of her old yearnings.

"You're so lucky being a boy," she concluded. "I wish I was."

He glanced at her with undisguised admiration.

"I don't suppose it's your fault, being a girl," he said. "And you do *dress* like a boy."

They smiled at each other and instantly a bond was created, something that went far deeper than the shapes their mouths made. Pandora felt a warm feeling inside and noted happily that the boy's likeness to Ewen went no further than his looks. However, she resolved to ask about that particular puzzle when the time was right.

"What's your name?" she ventured.

"Geraint."

She was pleased that he did not offer a second name, for she had always believed them to be unimportant details. "Mine's Pandora."

"That's a nice name. How old are you?"

"Twelve."

"I'm fourteen." He said it slowly, proudly. Pandora nodded approvingly.

"Two years older than me. Where do you live, Geraint?"

"In Brechfa." He pointed away through the trees. "A path there is, through the woods. Takes you straight there. It's a quiet little village. Not much to do really . . . you're not Welsh, are you? I can tell by your accent you're from the South."

"Yes, I'm from London. But I'm staying with my Aunt Rachel. She has a big house, back up the track there. It's called. . . ."

"Savannah," finished Geraint. For some reason his friendly expression had changed. He was staring hard at the float in the water and his face was grim.

"You . . . know it then?"

"Everyone knows it," he replied curtly.

"What's wrong? Is there something about it you don't like?"

He shook his head, forcing a smile.

"No . . . no, it's just that some people say silly things, that is all."

"What kind of things?"

"Well, you know . . . the woman who lives there . . . Miss Ellis, I think her name is. Her being so young and everything, when everyone knows she's as old as the hills. And the man that lives there. . . ."

"Ewen?"

"Yes, him. People say some funny things about him, too."

"Yes, but what kind of things?"

"Well, for a start. . . ." Geraint broke off as his improvised float slid abruptly beneath the water. "Got one!" he cried. "Didn't I tell you there were fish here?"

"Yes, but Geraint! You were telling me about. . . ."

"Never mind that now!" Geraint pulled back on his hazel switch and a small, silvery fish broke the surface of the water, wriggling and lashing its body in a futile attempt to stay submerged. Geraint jerked it unceremoniously out of the water and let gravity swing it like a pendulum into his outstretched hand. He dangled his prize proudly in front of Pandora.

"There," he announced. "That is a dace."

Pandora examined it dubiously. "Bit on the small side, isn't it?"

"Of course it's small. Dace always *are!* But fine little fighters, just the same. . . ." He removed the fish carefully from its hook and it flapped helplessly on his palm, mouth opening and closing in silent indignation.

"See here," said Geraint, pointing with a grubby forefinger. "This is called the dorsal fin . . . this one the caudal . . . the anal, the pelvic, the pectoral . . . and this line here, the lateral line. Helps it to pick up vibrations in the water, see. Like our ears pick up sound."

Pandora smiled. "You *do* know a lot about fish!"

He shrugged. "A bit, I suppose. Only what I've read in books. How . . . how long are you going to be staying here?"

"For the summer."

"Perhaps we can meet up a few times." He reddened, embarrassed by his own boldness. "I mean . . . only if you've got nothing to do. I mean, it's all the same to me. . . ."

Pandora cut in hastily. "It would be really nice!"

He stared at her, almost as though he had expected a snub. "Do you really mean that?" he asked her.

"Yes. Of course I do."

Geraint gave her a curious look, a kind of sad, wondering, lonely look, that made her feel very soft and tearful inside. She thought that she had never met anyone more in need of a friend in her whole life. It was an amazing thing, but she was finding it very easy to talk to him. Perhaps she recognized a similarity to her own problems of friendship in the past.

The fish gave a last energetic flip of its tail and shot out of Geraint's hand into the waiting stream, with a loud plop! With a yell, Geraint flung himself down and plunged his arm into the water but the dace was gone. Pandora laughed out loud.

"I'd forgotten about him," she cried.

"Me too!" They laughed together for a few moments and then Geraint looked at Pandora in that strange way again and said, "I like you. You're different from the others."

"Others?"

"The girls in the village. I don't get on with them, see."

"Why not?"

"Oh . . . they're stupid. Talk about me behind my back, they do. Giggle and whisper. Not that it's their fault, I suppose. They only get it from their parents. . . ."

"But Geraint, I don't understand. Why should anybody want to talk about you behind your back?"

Geraint picked up a handful of pebbles and tossed them carelessly into the stream. "People," he muttered. "They won't forget things. Not in Brechfa, anyway. Something happens long years back and they never let it die. They keep it alive by gossiping about it, adding little things that they've made up; oh, face to face, they're as nice as can be . . . but once you turn your back. . . ."

He stared down moodily into the water.

"That's awful! You mean that you did something wrong a long time ago?"

Geraint shook his head. "No," he replied. "Not me; my Mother."

He glanced suddenly at his wristwatch as though his memory had just been jogged. "I've got to go now," he announced. "I promised her I'd be back for tea." He picked up the fishing rod and carefully fixed the hook out of harm's way. They both got up off the ground.

"I should be getting back, too," admitted Pandora.

"Hold on a minute!" Geraint stood before her rather awkwardly, the rod slung over his shoulder. "I was wondering," he began. "Well, I was wondering if you were . . . doing anything? Later on, I mean. . . ."

Pandora shook her head.

"Well, then, perhaps we could meet up again. Tonight. Just to talk."

"Talk?" echoed Pandora. "What about?"

"Oh, you know. Things." He frowned. "It's good to have someone who's easy to talk to, that's all. Still, it's up to you. If you'd rather not. . . ."

He made as if to walk away but Pandora grabbed his arm.

"All right!" she said. "When and where?"

"Midnight!" he cried without hesitation. "And here! I'll meet you in the woods, across the road from your Aunt's house."

"Midnight," she echoed uneasily. "Isn't that a bit late?"

"It has to be that time. Gives my Mum a chance to drop off, see. And it'll be great fun! I like being out late because there's nobody to tell you what to do and creepy things happen. . . . Oh, I never thought. Can you get away all right?"

She frowned. "Well, I suppose so. There's ivy underneath my window; it looks like it would take my weight with no trouble. . . . Only, you *will* be there, won't you?"

He grinned, "What's up? Afraid of the dark?"

"No, it's not that . . . only . . . well, please don't laugh at me, Geraint, but my Aunt's house is haunted. I know it sounds crazy, but last night I looked out of the window and down in the garden; I saw a ghost, honest to God I did. He was. . . ."

"A little boy with no clothes on," concluded Geraint. "I know. He's quite famous around these parts. People often see him wandering along the road in front of the house. Seen him myself, once or twice."

"Weren't you frightened?"

"Funnily enough, no I wasn't. He just didn't seem harmful in any way, you know? And I've never heard of him so much as harming a hair of anyone's head. Anyway, don't be worried; I'll be waiting for you at twelve. Bye!" He began to walk away, then stopped. He strolled back to Pandora, leaned forward and brushed her right cheek with his lips.

She stared at him in surprise. It was the last thing she had expected. She felt a sudden tearing sensation deep in her chest. They stood looking at each other for a few moments, unsure of what to do or say. In the silence, the noise of the nearby stream seemed to rise to a thunderous roar. Abruptly, Geraint turned and ran away, up the slope into the bushes.

"Don't forget! Midnight!" he called back over his shoulder and then he was gone.

Pandora stood as if in a dream, staring at the still trembling leaves into which he had vanished. She put a hand up to stroke her face where his lips had touched, then glanced at her fingers, half expecting them to be coated with glittering magic. But she saw only ordinary, small, pink fingertips, trembling slightly before her gaze. She wondered with the slightest trace of astonishment if this curious mingling of emotions inside her was the thing called love, that everyone made so much fuss about. She had always believed it to be an invention of the cinema screen and the pop record, not a real force that might settle itself on the shoulders of an ordinary person like herself. In this belief, she had lived secure and unmolested by that hideous word that was used so freely with such little cause by so many people. In her experience, love was her parents, always fighting, drifting apart and ultimately clinging together again, through need. This was Pandora's blueprint for love and she had never wanted any part of it. But now, suddenly, here was this curious aching *thing* locked within her and she was lost and happy and frightened and sad. Some inborn instinct told her that through all the years of her life to come, she would never experience the same feelings again.

She turned and her feet, buoyed up by a strange exhilaration, carried her in the direction of home.

It was late afternoon. The shadows stretched themselves, long and angular, across the grey surface of the road as Pandora approached Savannah. She went in through the open wrought iron gates that were set deep in the high, untended hedge and made her way along the gravel drive, deep in thought, her feet kicking little flurries of stone as she walked. She was thinking about Geraint and the way he had looked at her beside the stream, lonely and eager to make her his friend.

She wondered how the children of the village could ever dislike such a pleasant, lonely boy.

Walking as she was, head down, she did not become aware of Ewen's presence until she was right next to him. He was standing in the path, barring her way to the front door, his face as impassive as ever. It was almost as though he had been waiting for her.

She stopped, smiled in what she hoped was a friendly manner. In many ways, she was frightened of betraying her fascination for Ewen. It seemed to her that his dark suspicious eyes could delve into a person's very soul in search of secrets. She noticed,

with a sense of suspicion, that one of his hands was held behind
his back, as if he was hiding something.

"H . . . hello," she said cautiously.

"Hello." His eyes scrutinized her mercilessly. She flushed,
stared at the ground. "Where've you been?"

"Out walking. In the forest."

"That's funny."

"Oh . . . why?"

"I didn't see you. I've just come back from there myself."

Pandora managed to summon the courage to stare straight
back at him.

"It's a big forest," she retorted.

He nodded slowly. "Oh, aye, it's big all right. Got to be careful, you have, wanderin about out there. It's not so bad if you
know where you're going . . . but if you don't, it can be dangerous. Got my traps out there, haven't I?"

She stared at him. "Traps? What kind of traps?" she cried.

"Animal traps, girl! Why, that's where I've just been. Checking through them. . . . Look here!"

With a quick motion he snatched the hidden hand out and
dangled something in front of Pandora's gaze. At first she only
vaguely registered what it was; there was a brief vision of grey
and red. Then her eyes focussed. She gave an involuntary cry of
horror. The grey furry thing that hung there had once been a
rabbit, but only the tattered ears told her as much. Its head was
a crushed, featureless wreck, thick with black, congealed blood,
upon which several large flies were crawling and buzzing. Ewen
began to advance slowly towards Pandora, holding the grisly
plaything before him, swinging it from side to side. There was
an evil, almost bestial, grin on his face.

Pandora backed away trying to speak, but her eyes were filled
with the image of the creature's shattered head and a wave of
nausea took her.

"Please," she gasped. "Please stop. . . ."

But Ewen came nearer, striding forward purposely, the ragged
bundle of death held before him, where it might brush against
Pandora's face with its warm, sticky embrace. The buzzing of
flies seemed to swell, reverberate, inside Pandora's head. With a
scream, she hit out at her tormenter with her fists and then broke
past him and ran for the front door, her eyes filled with tears of

revulsion. From behind her came Ewen's mocking laugh and then the rapid crunching of his feet on the gravel as he came after her. Frantically, she stumbled up the stairs and slammed her full weight upon the door but it did not open. She stood staring helplessly at it for an instant, lost in nightmare. Glancing back she saw that Ewen was already at the foot of the stairs. She hammered at the door now, with her small hands, sobbing and blind to everything but her hatred for Ewen and his loathsome game.

"Let me in!" she shrieked. "Oh, let me in, let me in, please, let me in. . . !"

The door opened suddenly and she half fell, half ran, into Myfanwy, who grabbed her by the shoulders.

"For God's sake, Pandora! What is it? What's wrong?"

Pandora shook her head desperately, tears blurring her eyes. "Ewen," she sobbed. "He . . . oh . . . he. . . ."

The full horror of the incident claimed her now. She pushed her face into Myfanwy's shoulder and wept hysterically, her whole body shaking with the force of her anguish.

"Hush now," soothed Myfanwy. "There, there, love. . . . Why child, whatever's wrong? Won't you tell me now?"

Pandora sat upright, her tears subsiding. She stared at Myfanwy for a moment. Surely the reason for her upset was apparent. Ewen had been only inches behind her when the door opened. He must still be framed in the doorway, the dead rabbit clutched in his hand like an incriminating weapon. She turned. There was no one in sight. Beyond the stairs, the lawn was empty save for the grass and the dying sunlight.

Ewen was nowhere to be seen.

Chapter Seven

Pandora stared moodily at the sheet of white paper that lay on the desk top in front of her. She had been sitting up in her bedroom for several hours, pen poised to write, but as yet she had not scrawled a single word. It was almost eleven o'clock and, out in the garden, a blustering wind was stirring the trees. Pandora chewed the end of her pen thoughtfully. She had promised in Paddington station to send her Mother a letter and that was just what she intended to do. But what was she to tell Samantha that would not cause both dismay and worry? She tried vainly to envisage her Mother, calmly reading about ghosts, mysterious bumpings and mutilated rabbits. . . . It simply wouldn't do. Samantha had been reluctant to allow the visit in the first place and if she was to get wind of even one of the unsavoury happenings at "Savannah," it was odds-on that the so-called 'holiday' would be over. Pandora didn't want that at all, especially as she was convinced that her parents' proposed reconciliation would be shattered by her premature return. Though her fears were probably ill-founded, she was determined to fulfill her role in the marital game. She had also become involved in the most perplexing, interesting and downright mysterious series of events she had ever encountered. Wild horses wouldn't drag her out of the adventure until she had followed it through to its logical conclusion. Besides, she had found herself a friend in Geraint and a focus for her fantasies in Ewen, despite the fact that he seemed to want only to frighten her. It was a fascinating twist that the two men looked so alike.

Of course, there was still the problem of the letter. She didn't like the idea of lying to her parents and, on reflection, she decided that it should be possible to compose an acceptable piece of writing, simply by leaving out the unsuitable details. She thought about it for a few moments. It really did seem to be the best idea.

She picked up her pen and began to write.

Dear Mummy and Daddy.

Well, here I am, safe and sound, in Bryn Myrrdin! (Merlin's Hill.) I would have liked to phone you but Aunt Rachel doesn't have a telephone and the nearest box is miles away. You wouldn't believe how wild it is! There isn't another house within sight.

Aunt Rachel is very nice, very young for her age, too. My eyes almost popped out of my head when I saw her; she looked only forty! There is also Myfanwy . . . hope I've spelt her name right. She is the housekeeper. She is also very nice and a wonderful cook. She has promised to give me her recipe for homemade bread, Mummy, so I can make it for you when I get home! I think of everything, you see!

Today I went walking in the forest, a wonderful, big forest like the enchanted ones in fairy stories. Poor Aunt Rachel said she wished she could go with me, but her legs are bad most of the time. What a shame!

Guess what! I have already made a friend. He is called Geraint . . . hope I've spelt that right, too. He lives in the nearest village. (I won't even try and spell that!) He is very nice and good looking with it, almost as handsome as Daddy. I met him by the stream and he was fishing for . . . dice, I think he called them. Anyway, some fish. He caught one as well! Perhaps I might ask him to teach me fishing. I've asked Daddy lots of times, but he's always too busy.

Well, I'm afraid that is all the news for the moment. I will write longer letters when I hear from you. Love to you both and a kiss and two hugs each.

All my love,
Pandora.

She read the letter through carefully and decided that it would suffice. It certainly gave the impression that she was having a good time in Bryn Myrrdin and that, after all, was the main idea. Besides, it wasn't as if the holiday hadn't been enjoyable, up to Ewen's horrible trick with the rabbit. Even in that there was a mystery. How had he managed to disappear from the staircase in the fraction of a second that Pandora's back was turned? She sighed. However, it was done; she now intended to keep out of his way whenever possible. She remembered that she was to meet Geraint later that night. It would be fun creeping out in the dark, scary but exciting. It was odd, but every time she thought of Geraint, she experienced a warm, thrilling sensation deep within, a feeling that was totally new to her. Up till now she had considered boys—at least the ones she knew—to be rough and loud and generally not worth bothering with. But this one; this one had woven some magic around her, a magic that made her frail and loving, made her want to reach out and . . . touch him. . . . Yes, that was it. Touch him.

It was a strange thing, but whenever she thought of Geraint in this way, his image seemed inextricably mixed up with that of Ewen. She seemed to see them as one character, now young, now older, and she was unable to decide which aspect was the most exciting. Of course, her attraction to the older man could never amount to anything but, now that she had gotten over the horrible prank of earlier that day, she was quite surprised to discover that her initial admiration for the gardener had not diminished one little bit. She remembered the short dream she had experienced while travelling in the car with him. She had been disappointed to wake from it, even though it had frightened her a little. She had a fair idea of what was about to happen. . . .

She felt suddenly rather foolish and glanced quickly around the room, as though afraid that someone might have overheard her thoughts.

Smiling, she addressed a white envelope, folded the letter and popped it inside. She glanced at her watch. Twenty past eleven. She stood up and went over to the window, leaning out into the night. Playful winds snatched at her hair, fluttering it like a copper coloured banner. Against the inky sky a full moon burned like a great, ripe cheese.

There was a polite knock at the door. Surprised, Pandora pulled back her head and called out, "Who is it?"

"It is only me." Myfanwy's voice.

"Come in."

Myfanwy entered, smiling. Hello, there. Feeling better now?" Pandora nodded. "Much better, thanks."

Myfanwy was carrying a tray of fruit. "I noticed the light under the door," she explained. "A little fruit, I thought you might like. . . . You've not eaten one thing since you came in from your walk."

"That's very kind of you. Perhaps an apple, then. . . ."

Myfanwy set the fruit down on the desk and sat beside Pandora on the alcove bed. Pandora reached out and took a firm, green pippin from the desk. She bit into it thoughtfully. Then remembering the letter, she handed it to Myfanwy. "For my Mum," she explained. "I . . . suppose you'll have to give it to Ewen, won't you."

Myfanwy nodded. "Yes; but don't you be worrying about it! Like I told you before, he's not a bad man. He did not mean to harm you today, I am sure."

"But he did! You should have seen the way he came at me with that . . . that thing. He really meant to frighten me. It was a horrible thing to do."

"Oh, I don't think so. Probably just proud of his catch, really. Wanting to show it off to someone. A bit simple, he is; didn't realise you'd be frightened. Why, most of the little girls in Brechfa wouldn't think twice about a dead rabbit!"

"Perhaps not," admitted Pandora reluctantly. "I don't know. I just can't understand why you didn't see him, Myfanwy. He was right behind me when you opened the door. . . ." Pandora took another bite of the apple, then asked, "Has Ewen got any children?"

Myfanwy looked quite shocked.

"Of course not!" she cried. "How could he have? Why, not even married, he is!"

Pandora couldn't help smiling. "You don't have to be married to have children," she observed.

"Indeed?" retorted Myfanwy coldly. "In these parts you do! It would not be considered proper, otherwise. Whatever would people say about such a thing."

"It was only a thought, Myfanwy."

"Yes, well, such thoughts we can do better without, I am thinking! Whatever gave you such a notion in the first place?"

Pandora shrugged, said nothing. Myfanwy made an attempt to change the subject.

"How was your walk today?"

"Fine, thank you."

"Did you make any drawings?"

"No . . . oh, yes, one! I meant to ask you about it, too." She got up and fetched her shoulder bag from the floor on the other side of the room. The sketchbook was still inside. She took it out and found the appropriate page. "Here it is. What do you make of that, Myfanwy? It's obviously Welsh."

Myfanwy nodded. "It's Welsh, all right. Very old, though, I would say. The spelling is a bit different from what it is now. But it's a famous enough poem. . . .

When Merlin's Oak shall tumble down,
Then shall fall Carmarthen town."

"I thought I recognised the word Merlin," cried Pandora. "You say it's quite famous, then?"

"Oh, yes, most people know of it. In Carmarthen town, a stump there is, with those words written on it. Legend says that if the stump is cut down, that will be the end of Carmarthen, once and for all."

"No kidding!"

"But where did you come across this?" asked Myfanwy.

"There was an old tree in the forest, with a metal plate on it. It was written on that."

"Well, fancy . . . funny, it rather puts me in mind of the other poem."

"Which other poem?"

Myfanwy smiled at Pandora's curiosity. "It's an old poem in a glass frame. Hanging, it has been, on the wall of my bedroom, for many years. It seems that my room used to be the study of the old Master, Mr. Ellis. Very interested, he was, in old Welsh writings."

"I'd love to have a look at it," said Pandora.

"Well, I tell you what. I'm off to bed now, but I'll bring the poem up for you to see, before I turn in." She got up off the bed and went to the door. "Mind," she cautioned, "don't you sit up too late reading it. I'm sure your Mother wouldn't be thanking me for keeping you awake till all hours!" She went out. Her room was at the far end of the landing, just in front of the staircase, and she returned in a few moments with the poem. She handed the frame to Pandora. "You see," she said, "this one is about Merlin's trees, too. Only these are apple, not oak! Anyway, I'll leave you to read in peace. I'm off to my bed. Good-night."

"Good-night, Myfanwy. Pleasant dreams."

Myfanwy went out, closing the door. Her footsteps sounded gently across the landing. With interest, Pandora turned her attention to the poem. It was handwritten in a neat, legible style.

Avallenau Myrrdin.
(Merlin's Apple Trees.)

Fair the gift to Merlin given
Apple trees seven score and seven;
Equal all in age and size;
On a green hill slope that lies
Basking in the southern sun,
Where bright waters murmuring run.

Just beneath the pure stream flows;
High above, the forest grows;
Not again on earth is found
Such a slope of orchard ground;
Song of birds and hum of bees
Ever haunt the apple trees.

From the poem by Thomas Love Peacock. 1829.

Underneath this, in a different handwriting, were the words, "The Goblin Tree; Seven times with the charm." Pandora scratched her head, mystified. The latter was obviously not a part of the poem. She read the words aloud again, trying to derive some sense from them, but they meant nothing to her. "The Goblin Tree," she muttered. "Hmm. . . ." She suddenly remembered her midnight appointment and, glancing at her watch, she saw that it had gone to a quarter to twelve. Putting the poem aside for the moment, she put on her socks and shoes and then rummaged through the wardrobe for a thick jumper. There was little cloud in the sky tonight and the air had turned rather chill. Suitably clothed, she lay down on the bed and ate another apple, while she waited impatiently for the clock to approach the hour. She held herself back from going early, afraid that Geraint might not be there. She was loath to wait around in the darkness by herself.

After what seemed an age, the minute hand was standing vertical. She switched off the reading lamp and tiptoed to the door of her room. Opening it, she peered out onto the landing. All was in darkness. Carefully, she let the door close, wincing violently when it let out a terrible creak. Then she moved softly back to the bed, climbed onto it, opened the little window and peered out into the night. The drop looked terrifying and she very nearly gave up the idea there and then; but, after several moments' hesitation, she got up onto the sill, turned herself about and began to lower herself gingerly down, her right foot questing for a hold in the thick ivy and creepers that clung to the wall below her. For a few nasty seconds, she dangled precariously, finding nothing but leaves and air, but then her toes brushed against a thick woody stem and she let herself down a step, plunging her hands into the most tenacious holds she could find. Once, a handful of ivy tore away in her grasp and she had to stifle a cry of fear as she momentarily swung away from the wall. As it was, the rustling of vegetation seemed loud enough to wake the whole house. She hung where she was for a moment, her heart pounding, dreading the thought of discovery. How could she ever explain her actions at such an untimely hour? Luckily, it seemed that everyone was sleeping soundly. She continued carefully on her perilous descent and, at last, dropped the final few feet to the ground.

Breathing heavily, she consulted the luminous dial of her wristwatch and realised that the climb had taken her a good five minutes. She had forgotten to allow for it and now she was late.

Jumping up, she sped across the garden as silently as a ghost. She avoided running on the gravel drive until she was well out of reach of the house and, hurrying as she was, arrived at the gates inside of a few seconds. She stepped out onto the road, hoping to spot Geraint's attendant figure straight away. She was out of luck.

The moonlight bathed the grey ribbon of road in an unnatural glow, making it look almost silver, like the track of some gigantic snail. On its far side a dark forbidding vista of forest stretched itself away into the distance. Reluctant to shout and call attention to anyone who might be wandering about at such an ungodly hour, she crossed over and stepped cautiously into the trees. The moon seemed to go out as suddenly as an extinguished candle and she stood uncertainly in a threatening world of whispering foliage and metallic insect chirrupings. She swallowed with difficulty, but steeled herself to go onwards a little distance, glancing nervously this way and that. Everywhere looked menacing and distorted. Occasionally, the moon managed to peer through the canopy of green and send flashing slivers of white light onto the roots of trees, but this spasmodic effect tended to be even more unnerving than the darkness.

She allowed herself to call out in a hoarse whisper.

"Geraint? Where are you?"

If her new found friend was anywhere around, he was keeping quiet about it. She stumbled on, tripping over concealed brambles, and once, a feathery cluster of leaves brushed against her cheek, causing her to start violently. She paused for a moment, her back against a tree, unsure of what to do. Then a pronounced rustling in the bushes to her right attracted her attention. She breathed a sigh of relief.

"There you are!" she exclaimed. "Where on earth have you been?"

There was no reply. The rustling stopped.

She called out again. "Geraint? Is that you?"

No reply, but the hidden movement resumed, a slow, definite bending of branches and snapping of twigs.

"Geraint, that's not funny. Come out of there this instant or I'm going straight home! Geraint, did you hear me?"

With horrible abruptness a hand grabbed her shoulder from

behind. She spun around, a scream of terror on her lips, only to find herself looking at a smiling Geraint.

"You!" she cried. "Thank God. . . ." Her relief gave way rapidly to anger. "And what's the idea of creeping up on me like that?" she demanded. "You frightened the life out of me!"

He looked at her quizzically. "I didn't creep up," he replied. "I was waiting down that way and I heard you shouting to somebody, so I just walked up. Who were you talking to, anyway?"

"Oh, come on, don't kid me around!" she retorted indignantly. "It was you, fooling about in that bush. . . ." The impossibility of that statement dawned on her as the words left her mouth. Geraint had approached her from behind. The bush had still been moving as his hand grabbed her shoulder. "Oh, lord," she gasped. "There was someone in that bush there, moving about . . . and whoever it was, I was talking to him!"

"What?" He stared at her.

"Honest to God, Geraint, there was somebody. . . ."

Another violent shaking in the undergrowth made them both jump.

"It's probably a bird or something," muttered Geraint unconvincingly.

"A big bird," replied Pandora grimly.

"Well, let's have a look. . . ." Geraint took a step forward, then stopped dead in his tracks. A tall, angular piece of blackness seemed to detach itself from the source of the commotion and hurry off through the trees. The blackness was man shaped.

"There *was* somebody there!" yelled Pandora.

"Yes." Geraint waited uncertainly for a moment, then grabbed Pandora's hand. "C'mon," he suggested. "Let's go after him!"

"I don't think we should," reasoned Pandora. "It might not be safe. And anyway, I thought we were going to talk. . . ?"

"We can do that any old time," reasoned Geraint. "Look, if we don't go now, he'll get away. . . . Come on, Pandora!"

Reluctantly, she allowed herself to be dragged along in Geraint's insistent grasp.

They ran through rustling, forest shadow, hot and breathless with the length of their chase. Thin whip-like branches lashed at their faces and their knees were stinging from half a dozen falls.

Pandora was aware of her heart, pounding like a steam hammer inside her chest, but Geraint still pulled her forward through the night. Occasionally, some distance ahead of them, a crash of vegetation told them that they were still on the right trail. Sometimes, too, there were different sounds; a kind of guttural moaning that seemed hardly human at all, or an anguished howl like some animal in pain.

"For God's sake, Geraint. . . ." she gasped. "What's making those noises?"

He shook his head and she glimpsed his face, pale and grim in the darkness. Still he ran on and still Pandora was obliged to follow. The bushes thinned and the ground angled downwards. Below them, in a flood of moonlight, they saw the stream where Pandora had first encountered Geraint. A man was splashing through the shallow water, oblivious to the row of stepping stones beside him. He seemed to be in the throes of some kind of violent convulsion, his hands clutched around his throat, his mouth issuing a thick, white foam. Hideous grunting snarls escaped from his lips as he stood for a moment, swaying and reeling in the middle of the stream. Horrified, Geraint and Pandora came to a halt on the crest of the rise. From where they were, they could see the man's face quite clearly, a face twisted and contorted by pain into a mask of unspeakable suffering.

"Ewen," thought Pandora numbly. "But what's happened to him?"

She looked at Geraint and saw that his face was twisted, too, not by pain, but by emotion; his eyes were brimming with tears. He was fighting hard to keep from crying.

"Geraint!" cried Pandora. "What is it? What's wrong?"

He shook his head dumbly, pulled her forward again. She resisted.

"Why, Geraint? What's the point? We've seen who it is!"

"I have to know where he goes!" screamed Geraint. He broke away from her and ran madly down the incline after Ewen, who was now fleeing up the far bank of the stream. Pandora hesitated only a moment before plunging into pursuit, though her head advised her differently. She had to stay with Geraint now. Pause to think and she might lose him forever; he might run headlong out of her life, taking his warmth and comfort with him.

They ran now in incongruous, single file. Ewen, blind and raving, stumbling through treacherous thickets. Geraint, silent and tearstained, borne along on some quest that could not be denied. Pandora, frightened and losing the race, wanting only to keep the others in sight and vainly wishing that she was home in the warm safety of her bed. She went precariously over the stepping stones and followed the path up the slope, knowing only too well where it led. Somewhere before her, beyond the screen of trees, was the clearing where no birds sang. Distorted, old-men faces loomed out of the night, clawing at her with their skeleton fingers. She was vaguely aware of a stinging sensation across her right cheek and a warm trickle of blood. She dabbed at it with the back of her hand, but never paused for breath. She was running mechanically now, like an automaton, following the distant sounds of pursuit. A seemingly impenetrable screen of foliage barred her way and, covering her face with an arm, she leapt at it. For a few moments it held her fast, gripping her hair, snagging her clothes. She kicked and wriggled and fought her way through, emerging suddenly on the edge of the clearing. Geraint was standing with his back to her, his shoulders heaving either from emotion or exhaustion or both. Ewen was nowhere to be seen. The clearing looked ghastly in the light of the moon. Pandora hurried forward and touched Geraint lightly on the shoulder. She saw that he was indeed crying, quite soundlessly. She stood for a moment, helpless, then put her arms around him. He pushed close to her and she whispered:

"What is it, Geraint? Please tell me . . . why did you want to follow him?"

"Did you see his face?" countered Geraint. "Did you?"

"Yes, of course. It was Ewen, the gardener from my Aunt's house."

"He looks like me, doesn't he!"

"Yes, yes, he does . . . but. . . ."

"They say he's my Father!"

"Who says?"

"In the village. They all say it." He wiped at his eyes with his sleeve and pulled away a little. His crying had subsided and he looked a little ashamed. He stared away to the middle of the clearing.

"Well, that's ridiculous!" cried Pandora. "Just because you

look like somebody, that doesn't prove a thing. What does your real Father say about it all?"

"My real Father?" Geraint laughed derisively. "You don't understand. I haven't got a Father. I don't even know who he is. . . . People say that it's Ewen. They call my Mother a whore, do you know that? Fourteen years ago it happened and they never let her forget about me. It's a wonder she can bear to look at me. . . ."

"You mustn't say that, Geraint!"

He turned away from her. "Mustn't I?" he retorted. "You don't know what it's like . . . not knowing. Supposing that . . . thing . . . that we just chased *is* my Father. D'you think that's anything to be proud of?"

"Can't you ask your Mother who it was?" reasoned Pandora.

Geraint turned slowly around and stared at her. "My Mother," he said, "doesn't know that herself!"

"But how, Geraint. She . . . she must know."

Geraint shook his head. "She swore to me on God's bible that she'd never been with any man before I was born. A virgin, she was, right to the birth."

"But that's im. . . ."

"Impossible? Do you think I don't know that? D'you think I've not told myself the same thing, a thousand times over. . . . But I'll tell you something now, Pandora. She wouldn't lie about anything, my Mother. She wouldn't. She doesn't understand it herself. . . . If you could hear some of the things that the people in the village say. Overheard them, I have, talking dirt about her. . . ." He sat down on a horizontal tree root and buried his head in his hands.

"The Virgin Mary had a baby," said Pandora. "The . . . Immaculate . . . Conception, it was called."

He glanced up at her. "Do you believe me, then?"

"I don't know, Geraint. Ewen . . . you do look an awful lot like Ewen."

"I know," sighed Geraint. "But I don't care what people tell me. I believe my Mother!"

Pandora walked over and kneeled beside him.

"There must be some explanation," she said thoughtfully. "I live in the same house as Ewen; maybe if I snoop around a bit I can find out what's going on. . . . I wonder what was wrong with him just now. It was horrible. . . ."

"I've seen him like that before," muttered Geraint. "In the woods. That time he got away . . . but I know where he went now; I saw him." He pointed to the tall oak tree on which Pandora had discovered the Welsh poem. "Down there," he said. "Under the Goblin tree."

"The. . . ." Pandora stared at him. Instantly, Myfanwy's framed poem leapt into her mind and the final mysterious words, "The Goblin Tree; Seven times with the charm," seemed to jangle like bells in her memory. "The Goblin tree," she echoed. "Geraint, why is it called that?"

"Well, there's lots of old stories about it . . . how it belonged to Myrrdin, the wild man of the woods . . . and how in olden times all kinds of magic ceremonies were carried out under its branches; you know, witchcraft, black magic, that sort of thing. But most of all, there's a special thing that most people don't know about. I tell you what, if you meet me tomorrow, say about midday, I'll show you what I mean."

"Couldn't you show me now?" asked Pandora impatiently.

"No; it has to be at a certain time."

"All right, then. Twelve o'clock tomorrow." Instinctively, they both stood up to walk back in the direction of home. "It's a funny thing," said Pandora. "I was sitting right by that tree only this afternoon. Did you know that there was a plaque on it?"

Geraint shook his head.

"Well, there is. It's obviously very old and it's all covered over with ivy. 'When Merlin's oak shall tumble down. . . .'"

"Then shall fall Carmarthen town! Well, fancy that being on it! Everyone knows that there's only one Merlin's oak; and that's in town."

Pandora shook her head. "It looks like there are two now, doesn't it? I don't know why, but I've got a feeling that it's important, somehow . . . finding it the way I did and everything."

They pushed through the screen of bushes and descended the bank to the stream. They paused for a moment, watching the dark water's turbulent journey beneath the stars. Then they crossed over the stepping stones and climbed the far incline in silence. They were both deep in thought. They had walked several hundred yards along the track before Pandora spoke again.

"Don't worry, Geraint. I'm sure if we both work together, we'll find out something."

He smiled. "We can try," he replied. And there was hope in his voice now. He reached out and took hold of her hand, pulling her against him. His arms encircled her tightly and then his lips were upon hers, covering her mouth with warm kisses. They clung together fiercely for several moments; then a great gust of cold wind came driving out of the bushes, tearing at their hair and clothes. Reluctantly, they pulled apart and, hand in hand, they went on their way. Pandora felt immensely cheered now. She felt that together they could win against any odds. She let the thought warm and comfort her as they walked on through the darkness.

Chapter Eight

Pandora peered blear-eyed at her watch. It was eleven minutes past nine. She yawned and stretched, then winced from a dull pain down the left side of her rib cage. She had grazed herself climbing back in through her bedroom window. Pulling the sheets aside, she examined the wound gingerly. Several inches of flesh were scraped red raw. She decided that she would simply have to grin and bear it. It would be easy enough to ask Myfanwy for bandages and ointment, but the wound itself would be awkward to explain.

Reluctantly, she dragged herself away from the warm invitation of a couple of extra hours in bed and dressed herself in the usual knockabout costume. Then she went out to the bathroom where she brushed her teeth and splashed cold water onto her face. Once again, she was interrupted by some thudding noises from above.

"Beams," she muttered to herself. "That's something else that needs checking on!"

Refreshed, she hurried downstairs and found Myfanwy in the long dining room next to the kitchen. She was setting two places at one end of the huge table.

"Ah, there you are!" exclaimed Myfanwy. "Just thinking about giving you a call, I was. Miss Ellis will be eating breakfast with you this morning."

"Oh, good! I've hardly seen her since I've been here." Pandora sat down on a vacant chair and tried to suppress a yawn.

"My goodness," exclaimed Myfanwy. "Did you not sleep last night?"

"Oh, well, you know, I had a bit of a dream and it woke me up. . . . After that I found it hard to drift off again."

"Hmm. Bad conscience, I expect."

"What?" Pandora tried not to look guilty but was all too aware of a tell-tale redness on her cheeks. "What . . . what do you mean, Myfanwy?"

"Well, that's what they say, isn't it? A bad conscience keeps you awake. You've been up to some mischief, I'll be bound!"

"No, Myfanwy! Honestly. . . ."

Myfanwy smiled to show that she was only joking. "Just pulling your leg," she chuckled. She strolled over to the window and gazed out. In the near distance, a range of grey slate hills brooded in the morning haze, their peaks cloudy and indistinct. The sun was only just beginning to claw its way through the mist. "It's going to be a fine day," said Myfanwy. She went through into the kitchen and left Pandora alone with her thoughts.

After a few minutes, the dining room door opened and Aunt Rachel came in, supporting herself with the aid of a walking stick. She looked in worse health than when Pandora had last met her. Her face was pale and haggard and there were dark bluish sacs under her eyes, deep wrinkles etched into her forehead and neck. Though still amazingly young for her age, she seemed to have put on years in a matter of days. Pandora reminded herself that the light had been poor in the sitting room on that first evening, which probably accounted for the apparent change.

"Ah, Pandora. . . ." greeted Aunt Rachel. "We meet again. I'm sorry I wasn't around yesterday."

"That's all right! Here, let me help you to a chair."

"Thank you, my dear. . . . As you can see, I am somewhat at a loss today."

The slender fingers of the old woman's left hand closed around Pandora's arm in a surprisingly powerful grip, the long nails digging deep into flesh. Pandora had to suppress an exclamation of pain, but led her Great Aunt forward uncomplainingly, noticing as she did so, a vague musty smell that seemed to cling to her clothes. Oddly, the odour put her in mind of the time when she had climbed the rickety staircase to the top floor of the house and had pulled aside the wooden panel. It was the same ancient aroma of sickness and decay that seemed to grab at the back of the throat in a most unpleasant manner.

Instinctively, Pandora pulled away a little, but Aunt Rachel held her fast.

"What's the matter, Pandora? Something wrong?"

"No . . . no, it's just . . . my arm, you're hurting me!"

"I'm sorry." Aunt Rachel relaxed her grip but did not release Pandora, who was obliged to take the old woman onwards and sit her down at the dining table. At last, Aunt Rachel let go the arm and smiled engagingly.

"Here, sit down with me," she suggested. "Why, we haven't had time for a good powwow since you got here."

Pandora did as she was bid. Aunt Rachel sat regarding her in silence for a moment, a curious expression on her face. Then she asked,

"And what mischief have you been up to since I saw you last?"

Pandora forced a somewhat unconvincing laugh.

"Oh, no mischief, Aunt Rachel. I've just been wandering about, here and there. . . . I went to the forest yesterday."

"Ah, yes! Our beautiful forest. I wonder if it's still as lovely as it was when I was young?"

"I'm sure it is. When did you last see it?"

Aunt Rachel sighed. "Many years ago," she replied. "But I remember it perfectly. All those greens and golds!"

"Perhaps you can still see it," suggested Pandora. "If you can get hold of a wheelchair, I could take you along some of the easier paths. I'm sure it wouldn't be too hard. . . ."

Aunt Rachel shook her head. "No, Pandora . . . it's not possible, not possible at all. My doctors have absolutely forbidden me to go out of the house. The air you know . . . I'm very susceptible to colds."

"But the weather's glorious! Surely just for an hour or two wouldn't do any harm?"

"No," repeated Aunt Rachel firmly. "It's a fine thought, Pandora, most noble. But I'm afraid it's quite out of the question."

"What a shame. . . . Still, next time I go, perhaps I could fetch you back some flowers. I saw primroses there yesterday . . . and wild daffodils."

"That would be very nice."

Myfanwy entered with a tray full of food. In front of Pandora she set down a huge helping of bacon and eggs and toast; Aunt Rachel received a small bowl of thin soup, grey-green in colour. It looked most unappetising. Aunt Rachel chuckled, as though reading Pandora's thoughts. "It does look rather gruesome, doesn't it?" she admitted. "Myfanwy makes it up from special herbs. I'm afraid it's the only thing I can digest these days. . . . If I'm feeling exceptionally ravenous, I can just about handle a lightly boiled egg."

"How awful!" cried Pandora. "I don't know what I'd do if I were you. I really love food."

"Of course you do, my dear. You're young, and eating is still a pleasure. When you get to my time of life it becomes yet another . . . necessary chore."

Pandora chewed a piece of toast thoughtfully.

"Your time of life," she echoed. "And yet, you look so young, Aunt Rachel. I bet most women would give anything to look like you do at eighty years old. What's the secret?"

Aunt Rachel chuckled, an odd, broken sound. "There *is* a secret," she agreed. "And perhaps, before you leave, I'll share it with you. But tell me something, Pandora. . . . Don't you think that I look somewhat older than I did the first time you met me?"

"No!" lied Pandora.

Aunt Rachel shook her head. "You're being polite, of course. But it's true, there is a pronounced difference which I am well aware of.

"Why, I have only to look in a mirror and see for myself. Lines around my mouth and eyes. A certain sallowness beneath my cheekbones. A loosening of the skin around my neck. . . . Let me make a prediction to you, Pandora. Next time you see me, all those flaws will be gone. Wiped away in an instant!"

Pandora gasped. "But . . . how?" she exclaimed.

Aunt Rachel waggled a thin forefinger. "That is the secret," she said, "and so it will remain until I decide to share it with you." She went back to sipping her paltry breakfast. It was obvious that she could not be drawn back onto the subject.

Pandora's mind raced. What Aunt Rachel was hinting at was an incredible thing; the ability to defy the march of time, shrug off the years without a thought. Of course, Pandora had been astounded by her Great Aunt's youthful appearance on their first meeting. Now, only a couple of days later, there did seem to be a distinct change in her. Would she really be able to turn back the clock, as she had suggested? It seemed fantastic. Pandora thought of many of her Mother's actress friends, some of whom spent small fortunes every week in the countless beauty salons of London, in vain attempts to halt the accumulation of lines on their plump faces. How much would they be prepared to give for such a secret? And what form would it take? A tiny stoppered bottle of mysterious green liquid, perhaps . . . or a dark incantation muttered over a sulphurous flame.

She tried to imagine how it would be to stay the same age forever. It would certainly be no fun staying twelve years old for the rest of one's life. But one could wait for the best time . . . say, *twenty-one* . . . and then. . . .

'If only Aunt Rachel would let her know how the thing worked. She hated being kept in the dark about anything.

Aunt Rachel's voice cut across her thoughts.

"And what are you planning to do this afternoon?"

"Do? What? Oh, I'm sorry, I was miles away. I think perhaps I'll go for a nice, long walk again."

"I do hope you're not getting too bored by yourself. What a shame you don't know anybody hereabouts."

"But I do!" The reply had come out automatically and she cursed herself silently. She wasn't sure if it was a good thing or not for Aunt Rachel to know about Geraint.

"You've met someone, then?" There was more than a trace of suspicion in the question.

"No . . . no, I meant . . . I know *you*. And Myfanwy. And Ewen. You're all the friends I need."

"I see." Aunt Rachel seemed satisfied by Pandora's stumbling reply. "I thought perhaps. . . ." She gazed abstractly out of the window for a moment. "There is a village quite near . . . Brechfa . . . but I don't think it would be a good idea to associate with any of the children from there."

"Oh. Why not?"

"Well . . . they're a simple crowd. Not educated like you are. Some of them tend to get silly ideas about Savannah and the people in it. Just because we live alone, you see. Myfanwy has had some things shouted at her before now . . . wicked, hurtful things. Ignorance, nothing more! Of course, I don't wish to tell you how to spend your time . . . but if you should meet up with one of the village children, please be discreet. I wouldn't like you to be subjected to any hurtfulness."

"I understand," replied Pandora.

"Of course you do. You're a good child. Thoughtful . . . intelligent . . . I knew from the moment I saw you that you were the right one." She pushed her soup bowl away, hardly touched. "Well, I declare, my appetite gets smaller every day." She watched as Pandora finished up the last remains of a veritable feast. "While yours gets bigger!" she added wryly. "I can't think where you put it all."

"Hollow legs," explained Pandora. "That's what Daddy says, anyway!"

"Ah, your father, yes. Such a clever writer . . . something that I've always wanted to be. Some of his letters are very witty."

"Yes, he does have a sense of humour. I think so, anyway. But it's sometimes a bit hard to follow. . . . Mummy gets furious, you know, when she can't understand some joke he's made. Daddy loves that and he plays on it, tries to make her feel that she's thick. It can cause terrible ructions. Mummy's got a much broader sense of humour. She likes smutty stories. . . ."

"Really?"

"Don't get the wrong impression. She's really the loveliest person. All film people are like that, though; they don't mean any harm."

"I'm sure they don't. Has your Mother made many films?"

"Yes, lots. Her last one was really good, *The Acid Summer,* it was called. It was about this gang of narcotics smugglers in South America and Mummy played a kind of female secret agent who is hired by the American Government to pose as a drug addict and break the syndicate up."

"Indeed." Aunt Rachel smiled. "I must say the whole thing sounds fascinating. Is there . . . ?" She stopped abruptly in mid sentence and placed a hand against her forehead, as though dizzy. Her face seemed to drain of colour in an instant; then she was swaying over in her seat as if she was going to faint. Pandora jumped up and supported her arm. "Aunt Rachel?"

"One . . . one of my little turns . . . I'm afraid," mumbled the old woman. "Perhaps you can call someone."

Pandora yelled for Myfanwy, who came running from the kitchen. She seemed well accustomed to the incident.

"Dear, dear," she crooned. "Better get you upstairs, Miss Ellis. A lie down will soon put you right. Here, Pandora, take the other arm. I haven't seen Ewen all morning, devil take him! He's never around when he's wanted. Easy now . . . off we go!" Together they managed to carry Aunt Rachel along. She seemed to weigh hardly anything. They went out of the room and along the corridor with no problems, but getting up the long flight of stairs was a different affair. By the time they reached the landing, Pandora was out of breath and poor Aunt Rachel was moaning incoherently, something about Ewen. "Tell him to hurry," she croaked. "She's got out somehow; she's trying to make me take it all back . . . bring . . . Ewen . . . and the cat. . . ." Pandora glanced at her face and saw that it was haggard and lined with pain; or was it something more than that? She paused for a moment and stared in utter disbelief. If Aunt Rachel had looked forty years old at their first meeting and fifty only moments before . . . now she looked sixty. Pandora felt a numbness run through her. As she watched, the woman's face seemed to be aging, sprouting lines, collapsing upon itself like a dying flower.

"Myfanwy," she shrieked. "What's happening to her?"

"Nothing, girl." Myfanwy's voice was grim, calm. "It's just a dizzy spell, that is all."

"But her face . . . she's getting older."

"Nonsense. The light here is bad; you're imagining things. Hurry up now!"

They stumbled along. Pandora kept glancing at her Great Aunt, trying to reassure herself that she was mistaken. But the face kept changing, clawing in upon itself like melting wax. And the old woman was sixty-five . . . seventy. . . . They reached the door to Aunt Rachel's bedroom and Myfanwy almost kicked it open. Then she picked the old woman up like a limp doll in her arms and hurried inside. "Stay here," she said, but instinctively Pandora followed. She found herself in complete darkness.

The room felt like the inside of some mountain cave. It was icy cold and damp. Pandora strained her eyes but nowhere was there the faintest glimpse of daylight. Ahead of her, she heard the soft creak of bedsprings as Aunt Rachel was released from Myfanwy's grasp. Pandora reached out her hand to touch the near side wall and instantly withdrew it with a cry of revulsion. Her fingers were coated with what felt like a thick slime.

"Pandora! What are you doing?" Myfanwy's voice.

"I was . . . looking for a light switch. . . ."

"I told you to wait outside, girl! Now go on!"

Obediently Pandora hurried back out into the light. She glanced at her fingers and saw that they were covered with a kind of grey fungus. She pulled a handkerchief from her back pocket and wiped at it gingerly. Myfanwy came out and closed the door.

"There now," she sighed. "She'll be fine after a little sleep. Not eating enough, that's her trouble. What's that on your hand?"

Pandora frowned. "I'm not sure. Some kind of . . . rot, I think. It was on the wall. . . . Myfanwy, why didn't you want me to put the light on?"

"Miss Ellis needs complete darkness when she is in a state. Covered with black velvet they are, all of the windows."

"It happens often, then?"

"Now and again." Myfanwy led the way downstairs. Pandora followed.

"You know," she said, "it really did look as though . . . well, as though she was getting older."

Myfanwy paused and looked back. "Ridiculous," she retorted. "I am thinking it's too good an imagination you've got."

"Yes . . . yes, I suppose you're right."

"Let's have a nice cup of tea, shall we?"

"Yes. I think that's a very good idea."

Silently, they made their way back down to the kitchen.

Pandora strolled along the drive. It was ten to twelve, time for her meeting with Geraint. She was carrying her sketchbook in the canvas shoulder bag, for such was her excuse for going out. Glancing back once, she noticed Myfanwy watching from one of the upstairs windows. She waved energetically and Myfanwy disappeared from sight.

"Nosey old devil," thought Pandora, smiling. She remembered Aunt Rachel's words about not associating with any village children. She sighed. It was a bit late worrying about that now. She found herself wondering about the old woman's mysterious "turn" and whether she really had been aging rapidly, there on the landing. In the gloomy half light it had seemed horribly real but now, in the calmness of reason, it did seem more likely that she had imagined it all. But, she reasoned, what about that horrible dark room, with its damp, rotting walls? She certainly hadn't imagined that.

As she passed through the gateway, she saw Geraint waiting across the road in the shadow of the trees. He smiled and came over to her.

"Hello," he said. "You're right on time."

"Good. Which way do we go?"

"Follow me." He led her to the right, up the road, away from the forest depths. They walked for some minutes in silence, each locked up in his own thoughts. They rounded a bend in the road and the trees ended abruptly on the edge of a wide grass meadow. Beyond it, in the middle distance, the land rose sharply and became a massive, boulder-strewn hill, several hundred feet in height, the top of which was shrouded in grey mist. Pandora let out a gasp of surprise. She had not realised that such a hill lay so near, screened as it was by the dense belt of forest between it and "Savannah."

"Bryn Myrrdin," announced Geraint.

"Of course! Somehow it never occurred to me that there would actually be a *hill* here."

Geraint grinned. "What else?" he demanded.

"Well, I know it sounds funny," reasoned Pandora. "But it's not always so you know . . . I mean, there isn't a circus in Piccadilly, is there? At least, not a real one with clowns and things. And you take our neighbours, back home. Their house is called 'The Willows' . . . and not a single tree in sight!"

"Well, all right," chuckled Geraint. He indicated a stile which gave access to the meadow and they clambered over. "But that really is Myrrdin's Hill . . . and that's where we're going!"

"Right up there?" cried Pandora.

"Well, about halfway up. It's a bit of a stiff climb, but not too difficult, really." He led the way across the grass, striding easily. Pandora hastened after him.

"This Myrrdin fellow . . . who exactly was he, Geraint? I mean, everyone tells me Merlin. Is that the same Merlin of the 'King Arthur' stories?"

"Of course! Do you know of any other?"

"Well . . . no."

"Most historians agree that the old stories are linked. I've read quite a bit about it. See, at school once, we did this project. We had to find out all about the village and its places of interest. Myrrdin was an old bard . . . a poet or writer . . . who lived in the sixth century. Many people believe that when the stories of Arthur were being written down, a long time after his death, the writers were remembering about Myrrdin and his deeds. He's sometimes called Ambrosius in the old stories. Or sometimes . . . the boy without a Father."

Pandora glanced at Geraint and saw that his face was grim now, the familiar, troubled look in his eyes.

"What are you trying to say, Geraint?"

"Well, nothing really . . . except that it's a bit funny how . . . see, some of the stories say that Myrrdin was the son of the devil. . . ."

"Geraint!"

"No, listen. His Mother was supposed to be a nun and his Father, an incubus."

"A what?"

"An incubus. It's like a spirit thing that gets into women's rooms when they're asleep and . . . gives them children, you know, goes with them just as a man would."

"But, Geraint, that's just a superstitious old tale. Things like that can't really happen, surely?"

Geraint shook his head. "I'm not saying that they can, am I? It's just funny, that's all. . . . Makes you think. Myrrdin was found in Carmarthen, too. It's all in the old books."

"Perhaps," admitted Pandora. "But you mustn't go believing that kind of thing, Geraint. It would be enough to send you barmy."

"I didn't say I believed it," muttered Geraint.

"Well, I think you do!"

"What if I did? It would make some sense at least . . . an answer, it would be, if nothing else. Can you think of any other explanation?"

"I . . . no, not at the moment. But I'm sure there must be one. I mean, a *real* explanation, not a lot of mumbo jumbo. Nobody in their right mind could believe what you just told me."

"The people in the village do!"

Pandora stopped walking and stared at him. "I can't believe that," she replied.

"They do!" Geraint grabbed her arm and there was a wild, feverish look in his eyes. "I've seen them, Pandora. The older people, mostly. When they pass me on the street, they make the *sign of the cross!*"

They stood looking at each other in silence for a moment. Then Geraint broke away and continued on towards Bryn Myrrdin. Pandora could not move at first. She was stunned by what Geraint had said. With an effort, she ran after him.

"Geraint," she called. "Are you telling me the truth?"

"Yes."

"Do you swear, Geraint?"

He stopped again and turned to look her in the face. "I swear to God," he replied. "I'm telling you the truth."

She nodded. "I believe you," she said. "But, Geraint, those wicked, wicked people!"

He shrugged. "They're not wicked. They believe what they believe, that is all. Like I said, it's the old people mostly. The ones that remember the ancient stories. Sometimes I can't help but wonder if they might be right."

"Don't talk like that," cried Pandora.

They continued on their way.

The meadowland was now inclining steeply and walking demanded more effort. After a few minutes they crossed over a low, rock wall and the ground became rougher. Pandora stared up towards the hidden summit. It looked a daunting prospect.

"Uphill all the way now," announced Geraint cheerfully. "But we've got plenty of time."

"I hope it's worth the effort," said Pandora, with a sigh.

They reached the broad grassy ledge at about two o'clock.

"This should be O.K.," said Geraint.

Pandora collapsed in a heap. She was totally exhausted, her arms and legs aching in every joint. Geraint, on the other hand, seemed in fine form.

"It does knock you out a bit at first," he admitted. "I come up here quite often, so I suppose I'm used to it." He sat down cross-legged beside Pandora and gazed away into the distance. She folowed the line of his vision and was momentarily surprised by what she saw. Far below, across the fields, a grey ribbon of road led into the forest and she could just discern "Savannah," looking for all the world like a tiny scale model. Beyond, the forest stretched, like an even grey-green carpet, into the middle distance. Further to the right of Pandora's vision, the uniformity of foliage was broken by a small picturesque village.

"Brechfa," muttered Geraint.

"I didn't realise how high we'd climbed. What a fantastic view . . . but what about the tree, Geraint? I thought we'd come to see that."

"There it is." Geraint pointed, directing Pandora's eyes to the very centre of the forest. In the distance she could see, quite plainly, a long, bare tree trunk, sticking up some twenty feet or more above the greenery. There was not a single branch on it and it resembled a totem more than anything else, its summit being a curious round knot of wood.

"Well," exclaimed Pandora. "I think I can honestly say that I've never seen anything like that."

"Just wait. You've seen nothing yet. What time do you make it?"

"Ten past two."

"Hmm. It's much too early. About three o'clock it should start to show."

"What should?"

"The thing I brought you to see."

"I must say, you're being very mysterious about it all. Can't you tell me what it's all about?"

Geraint shook his head. "Wait and see," he replied. "It'll be worth it."

Pandora smiled. "All right, then. But what will we do in the meantime?"

Geraint grinned. "We'll think of something," he said. He reached out his hand and began to toy with Pandora's hair al-

78

most absentmindedly. He was staring at her in that curious, longing way of his and she was abruptly reminded of her dream of Ewen. A tense excitement sprang up within her and she found it hard to control her breathing. Geraint moved closer, his gaze fixed hard into her own eyes.

She opened her mouth to speak but then his lips were on hers and he was pushing her down against the sweet grasses of Bryn Myrrdin.

It was about three fifteen.

For over an hour they had lain together on the ledge, exploring each other's bodies with increasing confidence. Only some last inexplicable fear held Geraint back from taking the final step. Gazing up through half-closed eyes, Pandora could see the hesitation mirrored in his face; she wanted him to go on, to release the pent-up frustration inside her and make her a woman, but she too was frightened of the unknown. They lay for a time, letting their excitement gradually subside, saying nothing to each other. They were both fully aware of each other's doubts.

Then, suddenly, the atmosphere changed. There was a bleak greyness in the air, the kind of electric intensity that manifests itself a few moments before a storm breaks. Geraint seemed almost relieved as he leapt up and cried, "Look, it's starting now!"

Pandora studied the tall, bare trunk in silence for a few moments. The sun was declining in the West now, causing black angular shadows to form along the pale wood, where certain knots and protrusions had formed themselves on the bark. It seemed to Pandora that these shadows were gradually forming themselves into a very definite pattern.

"Do you see it?" murmured Geraint.

"I . . . see *something* . . . but I'm not quite sure what it is. . . . Oh! Wait a moment. *Now* I see!"

As if by magic, the shadows had arranged themselves into the form of a figure, the figure of a short, elfin-like man, wearing a long, baggy tunic and a tall, wide-brimmed hat.

"That's amazing!" whispered Pandora, as though afraid that the sound of her voice might frighten the apparition away. "How long have you known about this, Geraint?"

"Oh, years," he replied. "Like I told you, come up here very often, I do. One day I was just looking at the tree and it happened. Mind you, this is the only place it happens that way. I mean, I've watched it from lots of places but only here does it do that."

"Do many people know about it."

"I don't think so . . . at least, I've never heard anybody mention it."

The image on the tree was still well-defined. Pandora took out her sketchbook and a pencil. She began to draw the figure in every detail. Geraint looked over her shoulder approvingly.

"That's very good," he said.

"Thanks. Look, Geraint, have you noticed he's got pointed ears?"

"Yes. I suppose that's how Goblins are supposed to look. It's obvious that's where the name came from."

"He's pointing."

"Hmm?"

"His right hand . . . look, it is definitely pointing *downwards*, at the ground."

Geraint shrugged. "So what?" he murmured.

"I don't know; but it must be pointing for a reason. Just think, Geraint, we're probably the only modern people who know about this. Perhaps, in the old days, people thought of that figure as some kind of God. . . . Perhaps they used to pray to the tree, even made sacrifices to it. Can you imagine that?"

Geraint chuckled. "I'd rather not, thanks."

"Ewen disappeared by that tree the other night. . . . I remember you saying he'd gone down, underneath it. Maybe that pointing hand is supposed to lead the way to something. . . ."

She sketched in the last details of the little man's face and then studied the finished picture in thoughtful silence.

"It can't be a coincidence," she concluded at last. "I think we should take a good, long look at that tree; find out just exactly where it was Ewen disappeared to. . . ."

"I don't think it's a very good idea," interrupted Geraint. "Anything could be down there. Supposing we had some kind of accident; we might never get out again. And there's so many old stories about that tree, you wouldn't believe!"

"Nonsense! If we're careful, there's no reason why we should have any trouble. We're both of us smaller than Ewen, so there's no way we can get stuck. I remember seeing some big tunnel openings beneath the roots when I was there that day; and there's nothing more frightening in them than a lizard or two. . . . Of course, if you're afraid. . . ."

Geraint reddened. "I'm not afraid. I just think it's a stupid idea, that's all. I can't think what you expect to find down there. And it's all very well laughing off the old stories as superstitious nonsense, but I tell you this, nobody in the village would go exploring those old holes if you paid them."

"Oh, but Geraint, you must admit it's a bit daft! It's only an old tree, after all. What could possibly be the harm in looking around?"

"Any number of things, Pandora. I just don't want to find out the hard way."

Pandora closed the sketchbook and slipped it into her shoulder bag. She glanced at Geraint rather disdainfully. "Just as you like," she sighed. "But perhaps you could lend me a torch. . . . I'm not sure if Aunt Rachel has one."

Geraint stared at her. "You're not going down there alone?" he cried.

"Well, it looks like I'll have to, doesn't it," replied Pandora tauntingly. "Since you're too afraid. . . ."

"I never said I was afraid!"

"You'll come, then?"

"I . . . oh, I suppose I can't let you go by yourself. If something was to happen to you, I'd. . . ."

"You'd what?"

"Never forgive myself! But listen, if we get into trouble, just don't come crying to me about it."

Pandora smiled. "I won't," she promised. She looked away again, to the distant shape of the Goblin Tree. The figure of the little man was now beginning to lose its definition, as the sun slipped down the empty sky. After about five minutes, it was gone altogether. A person, wandering the hillside now, and glancing out across the forest, would never guess what the sun and shadow had created only moments before.

"It's all like a dream," sighed Pandora. "A wonderful, mysterious, frightening dream. I keep thinking I'll wake up in a moment, back home in London and realise that none of it exists . . . Aunt Rachel, Ewen, the house . . . you. . . ."

Geraint chuckled. "I'm real enough," he cried. He offered her his hand and she squeezed it gently. "See, solid as iron, I am!"

"Yes, but then, dreams can be awfully real sometimes, can't they."

He shrugged. "Dunno much about that. . . . Here, perhaps we should be moving on our way. Getting late, it is, and it can be very cold up here when the sun goes down."

Pandora nodded and Geraint helped her to her feet. "Goodness!" she exclaimed, "I'm aching all over. That climb was harder than I thought."

"It's easier going down," Geraint promised.

He was right. It was.

Chapter Nine

They reached the gateway to Savannah just after five o'clock. Pandora arranged to meet Geraint at ten the following morning. "Don't forget the torch," she reminded him. "Oh, and bring some rope, too, if you can get it."

Geraint saluted her gravely. "Yes Madam! Anything else you'd like done? Trousers pressed? Boots cleaned?"

"Get on with you!" She gave him an affectionate peck on the cheek and he went on his way, with a carefree wave. Pandora went in through the gates and along the drive, humming tunelessly to herself. Ignoring the front door, she made her way around to the back of the house, where a small door gave access to the kitchen and an adjoining parlour, where Myfanwy spent most of her spare time in between her various chores. The door was unlocked and Pandora went in. The kitchen was empty and she found Myfanwy sitting beside a cheery, coal fire in the parlour, her podgy red hands outstretched to the blaze.

"Hello, love," she said. "Come and warm yourself a bit. Proper chilly, it's getting now."

"Thanks." Pandora pulled a little three-legged stool up to the hearth and sat down. "How is Aunt Rachel?" she inquired.

"Fine. Sleeping like a baby, she was, last time I looked in on her. It's a shame she had to be taken funny like that. I know she would like to spend more time with you."

"Oh, well, it's not her fault is it? Besides, I've plenty to do here, really; I haven't been bored for a moment."

"Good, good. Made any drawings today, have you. . . ?"

"Uh . . . well, I. . . ."

But Myfanwy had already taken the shoulder bag from Pandora's arm and was removing the sketchbook. "Ah, yes, now there's the little poem you found yesterday. . . ." Myfanwy turned the page and found the picture of the little elfin man. Recognition flashed across her face and she smiled broadly "Why, that's very good! she exclaimed. "How on earth did you manage to get such a good picture of that?"

Pandora frowned. "You know what it is, then?"

"Of course! Miss Ellis's charm. She never takes it off her neck, you know. It is very good eyesight you must have, to remember it so well and it being so small and everything."

"The charm. . . ." murmured Pandora.

Myfanwy slipped the book back into its bag and returned it to Pandora. "I'll make you some tea now, girl. I daresay you're hungry?"

Pandora nodded vaguely, lost in thought. She hardly noticed Myfanwy go out. She was remembering the last line of the apple tree poem. "Seven times with the charm." Could there be some kind of connection there, she wondered?

The back door opened and someone entered. Glancing up she saw that it was Ewen. He looked as though he'd been in a fight. His black hair greasy and windswept, and his clothes, torn and dishevelled, were marked here and there with patches of dried mud. His eyes were two black pits in an ashen face and he stood by the door and stared long and hard at Pandora, with an expression of unspeakable sadness etched into every line of his countenance. Pandora had never in her life been subjected to such a barrage of intense emotion. It seemed to ripple from him in great, crashing waves of energy and part of her wanted to run forward and comfort him, find out what it was that was troubling him. He looked somehow crushed and helpless, despite his dark, brooding strength.

He moved forward into the room, closing the door behind him. Pandora saw that he was carrying a small sack over his shoulder and whatever was in this sack was alive and moving.

There might have been a cat hidden within, because she thought she could hear an occasional muffled, mewing sound.

Myfanwy's voice shattered the silence.

"So, you're back then?"

Ewen glanced away from Pandora to where Myfanwy stood, in the doorway of the kitchen.

"Aye," he muttered. "I'm back."

"Miss Ellis is laid up in her room. You'd better not waste any time. . . ."

"*I know!*" Pandora saw Ewen's expression change abruptly, curiously, to a look of revulsion, mingled with a kind of sad, tired acceptance. Then, without a further word, he hurried forward, pushed roughly past Myfanwy, and stalked off through the kitchen and beyond.

"That man," complained Myfanwy bitterly. "Always throwing his weight around, he is." She returned to the kitchen, shaking her head, leaving Pandora alone with her thoughts.

"Ewen's being made to do something by Aunt Rachel," she thought. "I don't know what it is, but it's something he hates. . . ." She remembered the first thing that had made her doubt the normality of Savannah; the painting in Aunt Rachel's sitting room, supposedly painted by Ewen in nineteen eighteen. Up till now she had managed to convince herself that it was a mistake. . . . But had not Aunt Rachel herself spoken of a secret "fountain of youth"? Supposing that Ewen, too, knew of the secret? If such a fantastic potion existed, then he could indeed be old, as old as time itself. Were those dark, hooded eyes really at home in such a youthful face? She knew that all the various clues were bound up in one, all-powerful mystery. The painting, the boarded-up top floor of the house, the ghost boy, the poem, Ewen's midnight flight through a dark forest, Geraint's missing Father, Aunt Rachel's black, icy bedroom, the Goblin tree and, of course, the mention of the old woman's goblin-shaped charm. With a sigh, Pandora took up a poker from the hearth and began to stoke up the flaming coals until they blazed with renewed force. She let her eyes stare mistily into the orange glow, until her vision was just a blur, as though deep in the dancing heat she might find a solution to the mystery.

Suddenly, from upstairs, there came a short high-pitched shriek of animal pain. Pandora jumped up from her seat, the poker dropping from her hand. Turning, she saw Myfanwy standing in the doorway of the kitchen.

"What was that?" whispered Pandora. She was thinking of the sack that Ewen had carried up with him. "It sounded like. . . ."

"A rabbit," interrupted Myfanwy. "Ewen killing a rabbit, that's all." The reply was too pat, as though Myfanwy had been expecting the noise and had planned an excuse for it.

"Surely not! A rabbit wouldn't cry like that, would it? It sounded more like a cat to me."

Myfanwy shook her head. "No. There are no cats about here, only rabbits."

"Well, why bring it home to kill it, then?"

Myfanwy shrugged. "Who knows. Ewen is a strange fellow. We can't be expected to know what goes on in his head. . . . Miss Ellis will get better soon, I am thinking." She turned and strolled back into her kitchen, as though dismissing the whole incident from her mind.

Pandora stood by the fire awhile, listening intently. From somewhere above her, high up on the first floor of the house, she could make out the faint, repetitive clanging of hammer on nail. She shivered. Though the coals were blazing only a few feet away from her, it was somehow very, very cold in the parlour.

Geraint was waiting at the appointed hour.

He had managed to procure a powerful torch and a length of his Mother's clothesline. He was ill at ease, however, about the whole venture. As they made their way through the outskirts of the forest, Pandora told him at length of all the clues she had found. She had brought with her the framed poem, although she wasn't sure why. Some intuition had told her that it might prove of use.

"Do you know what really worries me?" she muttered.

"What?"

"Well . . . it's all been too easy. Finding out things, I mean. All the little clues lying around that could have been covered up. Only nobody's bothered to make the effort. Almost as though they don't care if I find out things."

Geraint frowned. "Doesn't make sense," he agreed. "If there really is something going on and you find out about it, why, bound to tell people, you are, when you get home. . . ."

"But supposing they never let me go home?"

He paused for a moment and stared at her. It seemed horribly quiet there beneath the trees, quiet and cold.

"That's crazy," he reasoned. "How could they stop you from leaving?"

Pandora didn't answer that. There was no need to. They carried on, walking.

"I think you've been watching too much television," continued Geraint. "But if you feel like that, you should get out of there *now.*"

"What? Leave before I've solved the mystery. Never!"

Geraint shook his head with undisguised admiration. "I don't know. You're a funny one, you are. . . . I can't work you out."

They fell silent again and moved on deeper into the forest. Soon, they were nearing the tight cluster of old men's faces that led the way up to the clearing. The trees seemed closer and more impregnable than ever, reaching out gnarled hands to snag clothing and scratch faces. It became an effort to make the slightest progress, almost as though these ancient sentinels were trying to bar the path to the most secret of trees. Pandora's imagination began to play tricks. Several times, she thought she saw branches actually *move* into her path and once, a thin whip-like tendril of thorns lashed at her face for no apparent reason. She said nothing to Geraint, realising that he was very nervous about visiting the tree. He had tried to argue that it was impossible to climb down beneath its roots and yet he knew full well that Ewen had done just that only two nights ago. It seemed that it was the unknown that he was afraid of. Pandora, an educated, civilised girl, would at one time have given no credence to the existence of ghosts and demons. Now, she felt her beliefs being moulded by this strange, barbaric land, where she was the outsider and superstition was rife. Perhaps she, too, was becoming horribly uneasy about what might lie in the damp, waiting earth. She swallowed hard. She mustn't show Geraint that she was worried.

They emerged suddenly into the clearing. Once again, Pandora could sense the chilling, alien atmosphere that she had experienced on her last visit. Before them, the thick, ivy-choked trunk of the Goblin tree beckoned. They moved hesitantly forward, neither of them wanting to take the lead at first; then Pandora got a grip on herself and strode resolutely onwards. And at last, they stood by their goal, gazing down into the dark, gaping wound in the ground.

It seemed as black and uninviting as the gateway to hell.

Pandora shrugged. "Well, here we are," she announced to no one in particular.

"Yes," acknowledged Geraint glumly.

She fixed him with a withering glance. "Hand me the torch," she demanded. He fumbled the instrument from his back pocket and passed it to her, obviously quite content to play a secondary role in this particular adventure. Pandora flicked the switch and directed a powerful beam of light into the opening. She crouched down to stare into the depths and discerned that the tunnel within appeared to end abruptly about six feet down. She was aware of Geraint gazing over her shoulder.

"Doesn't look much of a tunnel," he muttered.

"We'll see." Carefully, she slipped her legs over the side and dropped to earth. She glanced around. The opening was more or less cylindrical, veined all around with thick tree roots that would provide an easy exit to above. She glanced up and saw Geraint's anxious face, about a foot above her.

"Come on, Pandora," he urged. "Let's go. It's obvious that there's no way down there."

"Well, what about Ewen?" she argued. "He managed, didn't he?"

"Yes . . . well, maybe . . . maybe he just vanished through solid ground, like magic, you know?"

"Wait a minute!" She got down onto her knees and examined the walls at the very bottom of the pit. They were covered with a thick growth of weeds that might conceivably be screening something. She went slowly around the base of the pit, prodding with her hands. She had almost completed a full circle when, suddenly, her arm found emptiness and went in right to the shoulder joint. She gave a loud exclamation of surprise.

"What's the matter?" Geraint's voice, nervous, anxious.

"I've found something. An opening. . . . Geraint, see if you can get down here and give me a hand."

Muttering darkly about doom and destruction, Geraint made his reluctant way down and soon he was crammed tight next to Pandora, all ribs, knees and elbows. With great difficulty, she managed to direct the beam of the torch onto the place she had found. The opening seemed far too small to allow entrance; yet after a little probing, they found that the thick straggle of weeds was deceptive and, that with a little effort, a person might push through into whatever lay beyond. Pandora could feel a rush of cold air fanning her face as she parted the curtain of weeds. She directed the light of the torch into the opening.

"Crumbs!" she exclaimed.

Geraint uttered something a little more basic, in his native tongue.

Now the probing torch light revealed a long, gaping tunnel, eating its way down into the earth at a forty-five-degree angle. They could not see to the end of it; the light was nowhere near powerful enough.

"There!" cried Pandora. "I knew it." She glanced at her companion and his pale face seemed to shine like a tiny moon, beside her. "What did I tell you?" she cried triumphantly.

"You were right," agreed Geraint weakly. "Can we go now?"

"You *must* be joking! I'm not leaving until we find out what's at the other end of this tunnel."

"Somehow, I thought you'd say that," murmured Geraint. He watched helplessly as Pandora began to crawl in through the opening. In a moment, she had vanished into darkness and then he heard her curiously muffled voice say, "Fantastic!" With a shake of his head, he reached for the weeds, eased them aside and pushed his way through, into the tunnel.

Slowly, uncomfortably, they began their long and arduous journey into the earth. The tunnel seemed as old as time itself. Disturbed by the glaring light, it stretched its grey rock ribs around the two young explorers, like a hungry snake swallowing its lunch. In the lead, Pandora, her original bravado wearing thinner with every claustrophobic yard that she travelled. Her mind was now a riot of fanciful images. She saw herself entombed forever beneath the ground, hounded by huge, green lizards that appeared, grinning like ghouls, at the end of the tunnel. It was only her stubborn pride that kept her going. Behind her, Geraint, cursing the pain in his grazed knees, marvelling at Pandora's composure and bitterly wishing he were somewhere else. Anywhere else.

The tunnel seemed endless.

Pandora kept glancing at her watch at intervals of what seemed like hours, but the hands hardly seemed to be moving. They could not even be sure if they were still travelling down, or moving parallel with the surface or, indeed, angling upwards once again. However, after what seemed an age, they emerged into a chamber in the rock, where they were able to stand up. They stretched themselves with groans of relief. From here the tunnel continued, wide enough to walk along.

"Thank heavens for that," sighed Pandora. "Oh, Geraint, look!"

The beam of light had caught the walls of rock on either side of them. They were grey and smooth and veined like the skin of some vast reptile. Here and there a crystalline stalactite dripped water from the shadowy ceiling. It resembled the lair of some nightmarish beast.

Pandora glanced at Geraint and saw, by the grim expression on his face, that he was thinking the same as she was.

"If you like," she suggested, "I'll go on alone. . . ."

He shook his head dumbly. "We can't stop now," he said, in a voice that was barely above a whisper. "We've got to see everything."

Pandora sighed inwardly with relief. She wouldn't have had the nerve to carry on by herself anyway. Together, they advanced cautiously to the beckoning tunnel. Instinctively, their hands reached out and grasped each other tightly. And they went on. Where before it had been narrow and suffocating, now the tunnel threatened them with its very size. Gaunt it was, and hung with mad shadows that seemed to dance before the advancing light, like a tribe of rag-cloaked witches, assembling and reshaping themselves in the dark, forbidden recesses of midnight black.

Then, just as it seemed that fear had begun to conquer them, they saw light.

Green light.

The tunnel spilled into a large, open cave, the mouth of which led in turn to a land that was all green. But, for the moment, it was the cave itself that drew their attention. It was littered with debris of all kinds. Bundles of old clothing, moth-eaten books, the carcasses of what looked like rabbits, clay bowls and plates.

It was obvious that somebody knew of the place and, moreover, used it regularly.

"I suppose it must be Ewen's stuff," said Pandora. She crouched down and leafed through some of the books, while Geraint went to the cave mouth and looked out.

"Lord!" he said simply, and then fell silent. Dropping the book she was examining, Pandora hurried to him.

"Golly!" she cried, and found that she, too, had nothing much to say.

They were looking out onto a huge natural cavern beneath the earth, a cavern that was roofed with thick bramble-like vegetation. Here and there, at fairly regular intervals, huge trees reared up their trunks, their uppermost boughs seeming to entwine with the greenery above, as though to support it. Through the brambles came sunlight, diffused and coloured to a bright viridian hue, bathing everything below in an unnatural, lurid glow.

"Those trees. . . ." gasped Pandora.

"Apple."

"What?"

"Apple trees. See, fruit there is, on the high branches . . . but the size of the trees . . . must be two hundred feet if they're an inch. I've never seen anything like. . . ." He broke off, stared up at the high, green roof and snapped his fingers. "You know, I believe I know where we are; or at least, where we're under! We've come out under the old bramble thicket off to the west of where we started. Know the place well, I do . . . or, at least, I thought I did. Really thick with thorns, it is; nobody in their right mind would try and walk through it. And from above, you'd never guess there was something like this underneath. . . . Why, this is where old Gavin Thomas lost his whippet a few months back. I remember him telling the story. He was exercising the dog, see, and a rabbit there was, just jumped out from a tree. Well, of course the dog gives chase and the rabbit heads for the brambles. Next thing, a crash there is and the whippet is gone . . . 'like the ground swallowed him up,' those were Gavin's very words. Gavin tried poking about at the edge of the thicket with his walking stick and lost that, too. Said he thought it had dropped into a pothole! Just think, if he'd tried following the dog though . . . he'd have had a surprise! Mind you, people in the village never take any notice of what Gavin says."

Pandora had hardly listened to a word of this. She had taken the framed poem from her shoulder bag and was reading it intently. "Come on," she said vaguely. "Let's look for the stream."

He stared at her. "Stream," he echoed. "What stream?"

"The one in the poem."

He followed after her dumbly, as she threaded her way through the trees, marvelling at the colour of his hands in the weird light. They found an apple lying in the soft grass that must have fallen down from a bough prematurely. Even so, it was the size of a large grapefruit. And after a few minutes they found the stream also, winding in and out of the trees in a clear, bright flow.

"But how did you know?" demanded Geraint.

She handed him the poem. "Here, read it for yourself."

He read it aloud, adding his own thoughts here and there:

"*Fair the gift to Merlin given,*

"*Apple trees seven score and seven.* . . . Let me see now, that's umm . . . one hundred and forty seven, isn't it? There probably are that many, too!"

"*Equal all in age and size,*

"*On a green hill slope that lies*

"*Basking in the southern sun.* . . . Well, I'm not sure about that. . . .

"*Where bright waters murmuring run.*

"*Just beneath the pure stream flows,*

"*High above, the forest grows.* . . . It certainly does!

"*Not again on earth is found*

"*Such a slope of orchard ground;*

"*Song of birds and hum of bees*

"*Ever haunt the apple trees.* . . . Well, how about that! It does look like an orchard, too. The trees are too regular to be natural. Just think, we're probably the only people in the world who know about this."

"We and Ewen," corrected Pandora. "It's obvious from all the rubbish here that he comes here often. The thing is, why should he know this place so well? I tell you what; let's go back and have a proper look around . . . see if we can find anything interesting."

They made their way back to the cave, glancing around in silent awe.

"We'd better not hang about too long," cautioned Geraint. "Supposing he came back and found us here?"

"Don't even talk about it," suggested Pandora. They reentered the cave and surveyed the mess for a few minutes.

"I'll tell you what," muttered Geraint disdainfully. "He's not what you'd call tidy, is he?"

"No. It looks like a bomb hit this place."

Pandora went down on her knees and began to root through a sizeable heap of assorted junk. She noticed that things had been damaged; pottery smashed, clothing torn, wood splintered, as though someone had smashed them up in a frenzy.

"What are we looking for?" inquired Geraint, following Pandora's example.

"I don't know," she replied. "Something."

She sorted through a jumble of glass fragments and what looked like a collection of broken animal bones. Then, her eye was taken by a large book, covered in faded brown leather. She picked it up and opened it curiously. Inside, someone, presumably Ewen, had scrawled pages and pages of words in a curious, childlike hand.

"Hello, this looks interesting," she announced. Geraint moved over to join her.

"What have you got?" he asked.

"Writing. . . . It's all jumbled up, through. Bits of it are in English; but most of it must be Welsh." She indicated a large slab of spidery calligraphy.

"If it is Welsh, I can't make head or tail of it," he murmured. "What weird spelling! Some of it sounds more like Latin to me."

Impatiently, Pandora flipped a few pages, until she found a sizeable English text. Here the writing was extremely erratic, as though the author had been in some considerable stress at the time. It read:

"The bitch has become too fond of hurting me. She has realised that all she need do is apply pressure to the charm and concentrate her thoughts on me. Sometimes the pain drives me mad, such is its power. I foam and rave like a mad dog and wherever I flee, even here in my sanctuary, I am powerless to escape."

Then, once again, the writing became unreadable.

Pandora frowned.

"I've a good idea who the bitch is," she said. She turned another page.

"Look at this!" she exclaimed. They both read, their eyes wide with disbelief.

"I am Myrrdin of old, the sleeper beneath the soil, the guardian of the green land. I am the enchanter. In me are the old ways made eternal; through me is mankind made sovereign. Accept ye the faith of Myrrdin and rejoice ye that the ancient faith lives on."

"Fantastic!" exclaimed Geraint. "This book must be centuries old. . . . It probably belonged to the real Myrrdin! That would explain that weird language. . . ."

"Really?" replied Pandora. "Only one thing wrong with that theory, I'm afraid."

"What's that?"

"It's all been written in ball-point pen."

Geraint snatched the book from her and swore beneath his breath. "It's right enough," he cried. "Ewen has written this. He thinks *he's* Merlin! Christ, he must be a lunatic!"

Pandora stared off into the tall green trees beyond the cave. "I wonder," she murmured. "Maybe it's not so crazy after all."

"What do you mean?"

"Well, listen, I happen to know that Ewen is a lot older than he looks. Old enough to have painted a picture in nineteen eighteen, for instance. . . ."

"That might not be as crazy as it sounds," admitted Geraint. "There are old timers in Brechfa who will swear that he's lived at the old house as long as they can remember . . . and, of course, he wouldn't have to be Myrrdin himself. He could be a relative, a son of a son of a son kind of thing. . . . If we could only . . . Pandora, what's wrong?"

She was staring vacantly at the very last entry in the book. He took it from her and read through it slowly.

"I have seen the girl. Pandora, her name is. She is beautiful, everything I have ever desired. But the bitch says she is to be next and there is nothing I can do to change it. I want the child and hate her at the same time, for she is the means to the old one's renewal. Perhaps if I can frighten the girl, she may leave of her own accord."

Geraint frowned. He put the book down and began to speak.

"He's crazy. A raving nut case. You'd be best advised to go and tell the police. . . ."

He broke off in amazement.

Pandora was staring at him with an undisguised smile of triumph on her lips. In the strange, green glow of the cave, her expression looked positively malignant.

"He *wants* me!" she exclaimed, her eyes wide with exultation. "You read it, didn't you? *Ewen* wants *me*. All the time, I thought he never even knew that I existed and in that book he says I'm beautiful. What do you think of that?"

Geraint swallowed hard. He sat there, suddenly very much afraid and he tried to think of something to say. He sensed something in Pandora, a change in her character that was altogether unlike her previous self. She should have been appalled by the words she had just read. Instead, she seemed fascinated by them. He found it very hard to meet her gaze. In the end, the only words he could put together sounded weak and pathetic in the midst of such excitement.

"Let's go home, shall we?" he said.

"Are you crazy? We're just beginning to find out things. . . ."

Geraint licked his lips nervously. "That's just it! I don't like the sound of that last bit. What does he mean, *you're next*? Next for what?"

Pandora shrugged. "How should I know," she muttered irritably. "It could be anything, really. The only way we'll ever. . . ."

"Shhh!"

"What's the matter now?"

"Listen!"

"I don't hear any. . . ."

The words froze on her lips.

From out beyond the cave came the sound of somebody whistling a tune.

"Lord, who's that?" hissed Geraint. They listened intently for a few moments. The sounds were coming closer. Somebody was approaching the cave.

"It must be Ewen," whispered Pandora. She dropped the book and stood up uncertainly.

"Oh, God, let's get out of here," urged Geraint.

"Why should we? We've as much right to be here as he has!"

"Don't be a bloody idiot!" Geraint pulled at her arm. "There's no telling what he might do. He could murder us both and no one would ever know. Who'd think of looking for us down here?"

Pandora's bravado seemed to melt in an instant.

"Maybe you're right," she admitted. She followed Geraint into the rear of the cave. They reached the tunnel in seconds. Total darkness yawned at them and they hesitated for a moment.

"The torch, Geraint. I gave it to you. . . ."

"No! There . . . in your back pocket."

Reassuringly, the light knifed into blackness, seeming to momentarily alleviate their fears.

"Perhaps we should wait," suggested Pandora, forcing herself to be calm. "Maybe if we *talk* to him. . . ."

Behind them, in the cave, something fell with a terrible clatter.

"Come on!" urged Geraint. They took off.

It was a nightmarish run through the gloom, a stumbling, knee-grazing, head-bashing marathon, and they did not pause for breath until they were at the entrance of the narrow tunnel. Somehow it looked more gaunt and forbidding than it ever had on the way down. Once again, Pandora led the way, though she was by now very tired. Geraint followed, urging her to keep up the speed.

"I think I can hear him following us," he gasped.

They had travelled only a little way when disaster struck. Pandora, flailing out with her hands, inadvertently smashed the lens of the torch against an outcrop of rock and the light went out.

They paused for a moment, lost in total darkness, their breath sounding harsh and shallow in the silence.

"The torch," wailed Pandora. "Geraint, what shall we do?"

"Just keep going!" The voice, weird and disembodied, from behind her. Gamely, she began to crawl on again, trying to ignore the stinging of her grazed knees. The darkness was horribly disorienting. She could not even be sure if she was moving forward and although her common sense told her that the way ahead was perfectly clear, she found herself cringing from the expectation of banging into some unseen obstacle. She seemed to move on in this way for an eternity, her eyes straining ahead in the hope of seeing some kind of light.

"It can't be far now," she said. "We seem to have travelled miles."

"I just hope we can get out again," muttered Geraint, between clenched teeth.

The thought hit Pandora like a sledge hammer. She hadn't even considered it before. Supposing it *was* closed up somehow and they could find no way of squeezing out again. They would be trapped then, in the wildest place imaginable, where nobody would ever hear their cries. She cursed her stupid recklessness and promised herself that if she ever got out of this mess, then she would exercise a great deal more caution in the future. She wondered if Geraint hated her. After all, she was the one who'd insisted on dragging him down into a place where he had no desire to go and they really had very little to show for their effort. They'd found an underground orchard and they'd discovered that Aunt Rachel's gardener was either born in the sixth century or was a raving lunatic.

"I think he *is* Myrrdin," thought Pandora to herself. "He's certainly no madman. . . ."

What was it that made her accept the more improbable of the two alternatives? Something in Ewen's manner, a proud, gentle quality that seemed to simmer away beneath the surface of what some people might call insanity. Somehow, it was easier to attribute the evil side of his character to Aunt Rachel and her all-pervading influence.

Suddenly, there was light blazing into their faces and, joyfully, they scrambled the last few yards, pushed their way through the weed-strewn opening and up, into the fresh air.

They collapsed onto the grass, blinking violently in the unaccustomed sunshine and trying to regain their breath. It was as though they had climbed up from the very bowels of the earth; neither of them was in any hurry for a return visit. Even here in the silent glade, they felt far from safe. They arranged to meet at twelve the following day and then they hurried off in the direction of their respective homes.

The Goblin tree stood alone and mysterious beneath the watchful skies.

Part
The Second

Myrrdin's
Keeper

EXTRACTS FROM THE JOURNAL OF ALEX ELLIS:

November 11th, 1909

My hands are shaking so much, I can scarcely write. Today, fortune has delivered into my possession, something of inestimable value.

It all began this morning, with a tap on the door and an old farmer asking to see "the Master of the house." I was loath to see anyone at the time and asked the maid to get rid of him; however, after a few moments, she returned, saying that the old fellow had something that he was positive would be of interest to me. At length, he was ushered into my study, where he handed me a large, worm-eaten, leather-bound book. It had, he informed me, been wrenched from the earth by his plough, as he went about his duties. It was wrapped in several layers of cloth when he found it, much of this decayed and crumbling.

I glanced briefly through its ancient, yellow pages and, I declare, could hardly conceal my excitement. It was obviously *very* old, not printed, but scrawled in beautiful, faded calligraphy, doubtless worth a small fortune. I must confess that I had no qualms whatsoever about telling the old fool that it was of little value and, once I had given him a couple of coins for his trouble, he went away none the wiser.

November 12th, 1909

Closer examination of the book has led me to some amazing conclusions. The style and quaint spelling of the text, which is in the ancient celtic language, places its date of creation in or about the sixth century. The title of the book, too, would tend to bear this out. . . . Indeed, if I am to believe my eyes, it literally translates as, "The Book of Myrrdin"! Can it really be what it says? Certainly, I have no evidence to suggest anything to the contrary, and a swift perusal of the contents would seem to indicate that the book is chiefly concerned with prophecies and magic rituals.

My first concern now is to prepare a full translation.

November 27th, 1909

At last it is complete! It has taken me just over two weeks of constant work, during which I have slept and eaten little, so absorbed have I been. The book is certainly fascinating, a veritable feast of ancient occult arts. I know that many of our more "civilised" citizens would doubtless condemn much of the contents as blasphemy. Another interesting thing happened this morning; I finally discovered the charm to which Myrrdin refers again and again in the text. It was hidden in a small, covered recess in the cover of the book. It appears to be made of silver and is in the shape of a tiny Goblin. The discovery of it has set me thinking about the poem on page one, which I have translated thus:

He who wears the Goblin charm
Merlin's keeper then shall be.
He who Merlin's sleep doth break
Shall find immortality.
Seven times around the oak,
With the elf-charm in his hand,
Each time he must cry "Awake!"
Thus the wizard to command.

There is a tree in the forest nearby, which the locals refer to as the Goblin tree. Some of the more superstitious elements avoid it like the plague, saying that it is bewitched. It seems only too likely that this could be the tree to which Myrrdin (or Merlin) refers. Several times he mentions as his birthplace, Myrrdin's Hill. I certainly know of few other locations in Wales with this name . . . and certainly, none of them are anywhere near here.

I find myself seized with a reckless, almost childish urge to go out to that oak tree and . . . who knows? Perhaps I shall do just that.

November 28th, 1909

Well, it is done. Perhaps now I shall rest a little. I crept out late this evening and after several bumps and falls in the dark, I came to the old tree. There I solemnly strode around it seven times, crying "Awake!" as each circle was completed. Perhaps my imagination has become somewhat overwrought of late for, as I completed the seventh cry, I thought that the Goblin charm *twitched* in my hand, as though possessed of life itself. I confess that I was so surprised that I jumped a good foot into the air, almost dropping the charm. Shamefaced, I hurried home, praying that no poachers or courting couples had witnessed my little ceremony.

At any rate, what harm can it do?

November 29th, 1909

He is here. He arrived this morning as I was strolling in the garden, a young, black-haired fellow with piercing eyes. He just stood there, gazing almost sadly at the charm around my neck and said, "You called me. I have come."

November 30th, 1909

Ewen and I sat up till the early hours talking. (I have decided that Ewen is as good a name as any. I certainly can't call him Myrrdin or Merlin, after all!) He is not unintelligent, though he is unable to give me much information regarding himself. He simply tells me that he dwells in a land beneath the ground which is "all green." As long as I wear the charm, he will attend my every whim, though he asks to be allowed to return home on such occasions when I have no need of his services. Should I ever remove the charm, he shall be free to leave again. I confess that the last few days have been a source of puzzlement to me. Sometimes I wonder if I am not the object of some elaborate practical joke . . . and yet, I know it is much more than that. I have explained Ewen's presence by saying that he is my gardener. What use he shall be to me in the future, only time can tell.

December 4th, 1909

Damn my eyes, but I can think of nothing else! Immortality! It is written there in the book and I have talked with Ewen, who assured me that it is quite possible . . . but the price, the price! To subject a small child to the horror of living death. How could I ever condone such a thing? And yet, I look at myself in the mirror and see a debauched, ulcerous, old man, hastening to an untimely end. My heart has never been strong and I fear that the excitement of the last month has unsettled it more than ever. It surely would not prove too hard to find a suitable boy or girl. . . . The only condition is that he or she should be under thirteen years of age. Of course, there will be other restrictions. I shall be virtually housebound, for the power of the spell can only have effect within these four walls. Also, Ewen tells me that I may develop an aversion to bright daylight and I shall be required to eat regular helpings of a kind of herbal gruel, made to a recipe that is thousands of years old. When a body passes into the realms of the *undead*, normal appetite is lost completely. . . . But what are these small irks, compared to the benefits of immortal life? Lord, how I yearn for such a gift. Any sane man would feel the same motivation, of that I am sure.

December 11th, 1909

It is a God-sent opportunity. The boy came begging around the house this morning. I invited him inside and ordered the maid to bring him a meal. As he ate wolfishly, I asked him several questions. It seems that he has run away from his parents in Swansea. He has never got on with them and is quite sure that they will not trouble to look for him. He was quite near to exhaustion, so I had the spare room made up for him and sent him to bed. He is of no account and no one will ever miss him.

December 15th, 1909

Today, Ewen began work on a portrait of little Alun. He has told me that this is very necessary if our plan is to be a success. He went off early this morning and returned some hours later with a box of colours. I examined these and they were like no paints I have ever seen. They are housed in small clay pots and the pigments for them are derived from rocks and earth found in a certain area of the forest. To these he added nail parings and tufts of hair, which he had taken from Alun earlier and had ground into powder. The poor child can have no idea of why we required them; but this special "psychic" portrait will provide us with the perfect alibi for murder. Ewen has brought a small coffin into the house and this he has filled with a mixture of ingredients prescribed by the ancient laws of black magic. Over the coffin, he recited the words of a ritual prayer. In this unholy receptacle, as Alun dies, will grow a *Doppel-ganger;* a mirror image of the boy, perfect in every detail. Alun's double will live for only four days, then will begin to die, decomposing quite naturally. His body will be taken into the woods a long way from the house. Once found, his death will never be linked with us. This may seem like the ravings of a madman but I know Ewen, and I also know of the awesome power to which he is harnessed.

December 20th, 1909

Today, we prepared a room for Alun. We chose one on the top floor, with a stout oak door. Ewen treated the various openings with a kind of herbal grease which he has concocted. Once Alun is placed inside, the door must never be opened again for sixty years, when the boy's term of "life" ends. Some time after this, I, too, will die, unless I choose to replace Alun with another child in the same manner. Just think! Another sixty years of unblemished, youthful existence. If only it did not have to be achieved this way. Ewen's final act tonight is to hang the completed portrait in the sitting room. When it is done, I shall seal off the top floor of the house. The servants will be paid handsomely to forget that Alun ever came here.

December 24th, 1909

This morning we took little Alun and entombed him. It was horrible. The poor little devil was snatched straight from bed and he was still half asleep. Ewen carried him upstairs and flung him down onto the bed in the chosen room. Then we closed the door on him and locked it from the outside. Instantly, he set up a terrible commotion, screaming and banging on the door. My heart was heavy as I read the words from the book, the silver charm clutched in my right hand.

Undead spirit that sleepeth not.
Accept ye the will of Myrrdin's keeper.
Take to thy body every ill I pass on.
Take to thy body every line of age.
Take to thy body every ache and pain.
Take to thy body whatever I choose to bequeathe thee.

With that, a horrible silence settled, followed shortly by a low, hideous moaning. I felt a vibration run through my body, as though somehow I was changing from within. I realised that the transference was already beginning, that Alun was becoming a *referent*, a thing that has no form of its own and can only absorb what is passed on to it. Overcome with revulsion, I hurried away. Ewen then did the final thing, an action he calls, "Putting the watcher at the gate." I could not bear to watch. Surely, we have done some unforgivable things over the last few days but somehow, this one simple act served to grieve me more directly than anything else. The sound of Ewen's hammer seemed to ring throughout the house. Still, it is over now. Every detail of the ritual has been obeyed. That for which I have yearned is now mine.

January 6th, 1910

I don't think I can bear it any longer. The process has worked, there is no denying it . . . but am I to be haunted forever by the cries of the child? Ewen tells me to be patient, that it must cease in time. But I never thought it would be like this. Yes, I am younger, the pains have lifted from my body, but who shall ever ease the pains in my mind? God, help me! Grant me strength to decide. . . . Ewen has warned me of the consequences of opening that door before time. . . . I don't know. . . . I don't know anymore. . . .

EXTRACT FROM THE DIARY OF RACHEL ELLIS:

February 17th, 1912

I had the dream again last night.

I swear that it will make a madwoman of me before long. Always it follows the same pattern: the entry of the boy, whose portrait hangs in the sitting room mocking me day by day. Why can't I bring myself to destroy the thing? And the book, appearing in a recess in the wall above the fireplace . . . though this time, it seemed that there were two books, a smaller one, written in English, and the huge, black volume, in a language that I cannot comprehend.

I know that they are there, behind the portrait, hidden in the damp and peeling plaster on the wall; part of me is fascinated by it all, urges that I should examine the wall and remove any contents; another part warns me to be cautious, reminding me what curiosity did to the cat . . . but I have burned my hands so many times. When all is said and done, don't I *enjoy* having my fingers burned?

Certainly one thing is sure. Of the two parts of Rachel Ellis's soul, black and white, the latter is fighting a losing battle. I must learn the truth!

Chapter Ten

The night was as black and deep as a bottomless pit.

Pandora lay awake and nervous in the alcove bed, the blankets drawn up above her head. She was wary of sleep where nightmares lurked on the edge of consciousness, in the formless guise of half-seen, gibbering monsters; and yet, she knew also that here in the old, crumbling house, there existed mysteries every bit as perplexing.

She thought of what had been written in Ewen's book. She was confused. The thought that he admired her caused a strange, exhilarating stirring within, but as Geraint had pointed out, the wording was very cryptic. If indeed "the bitch" was Aunt Rachel, then it was the old woman, and not Ewen, who meant her harm. But why? And how was it possible for her to hurt Ewen by using the charm? Was that the thing that had transformed him into a blind, raving animal, that night in the forest? One thing was for sure; when Ewen had pursued her with the carcass of the rabbit, he had been only trying to scare her away in order to save her . . . but from what? There were so many questions crashing about in her head and she was unable to answer a single one.

Around the ancient bricks of Savannah, a cold wind howled and the building seemed to shift slightly, with a creak of protest. To Pandora's strained imagination, it sounded as though a voice was calling out her name, rising and falling with the stirring of the wind; a child's voice, high and sweet. Shivering, she pulled the blankets tight around her, trying to close off her mind to the torrent of nagging doubts that assailed her.

A gust of wind tore in through the open window, flapping the curtains and seeming to chill Pandora's body, even through the thick layer of blankets.

Impulsively, she sat up and reached out to close it. Her attention was caught by a patch of whiteness far below. She hesitated a moment, then peeped cautiously out.

The ghost boy was standing below her window, staring up at her, a curious smile on his face. As before, he was naked and the wind was blowing his tousled hair wildly about. After the momentary shock of seeing him there, Pandora's fear subsided and was replaced by a curiously calm sensation. Something in the boy's smile comforted her, set her troubled mind at rest. She thought of calling out to him, but was afraid that the spell would be broken by the noise, that he would vanish. So instead, she returned his smile. He nodded, as though to indicate that he was aware of her feelings. Then, he extended one arm and pointed up above Pandora's head. He seemed to be trying to convey something to her. She leaned out and glanced up in the direction he indicated, but could only see the upper story of the house looking bleak and foreboding against the night sky. She looked back to the boy and shrugged expressively. He remained pointing as before and once again she studied the front of the house, trying to fathom his meaning. Then, in one of the windows over to her right, she discerned some kind of movement and also a faint, luminous glow. She concentrated her attention on this, but the abrupt angle made it difficult to make out properly. There seemed to be a vague shape weaving to and fro beyond the glass but she could not be sure of this. For the third time, she turned back to look for the boy but this time, he was gone.

She frowned. She had already promised herself a closer look at that mysterious top floor, but it would have to be done at night, when everyone was asleep. She'd have to get hold of another torch somehow, for Geraint's had been left broken and useless, in the middle of the tunnel. With a sigh, she closed the window and lay down again, wondering who the ghost boy was and what caused him to be forever wandering the grounds of Savannah.

For some reason, she felt sure that he was an ally, that he meant her no harm. She hoped that her reasoning was correct. Another enemy was the last thing she needed.

She applied herself once again to the pursuit of sleep. It was a long time before she caught up with it. Dawn was anointing the western sky with gold when she finally discovered a hole in her thoughts and slipped gently into it.

She opened her eyes.

Morning was a confusion of sounds and smells. Myfanwy, down in the scrubbed, shining kitchen, sang a happy melody, rattling her own rhythmic accompaniment on a variety of pots and pans; out in the garden, Ewen, a stolid, human metronome, was working on the huge woodpile with his two-handed axe. The delicious scent of frying bacon seemed to fill the house with its tempting aroma.

Pandora sighed. The dark happenings of the previous day seemed distant already. She flung her blankets aside and looked out of the window. The abundance of sun belied the stormy, blustering weather of only a few hours earlier. Now the world was at peace with itself and its fellow creatures.

She dressed herself, then went out to the bathroom and splashed cold water on her face, until every nerve jangled. She didn't even glance up at the thumping noises overhead; she heard them every time she was in there and was getting quite used to the phenomenon. It occurred to her suddenly that the upper-story window to which the ghost boy had pointed the previous night, would be directly over the bathroom. She brushed her teeth thoughtfully. It did look as though she was destined to snoop around there in the near future, though she didn't much relish the idea. She remembered the disquieting feeling she had experienced by simply standing at the top of the stairs; and besides, after her misadventures in the tunnel, the thought of entering another place of darkness was far from inviting. Yet, despite herself, she made a mental note to ask Geraint about another torch when she saw him at midday.

She made her way down the stairs and followed the smell of cooking. She was more than a little surprised to find Aunt Rachel sitting in the long dining room, firstly, because she had never seen the old woman up so early in the morning and secondly, because Aunt Rachel seemed to have changed almost beyond recognition. Now, she was younger looking than ever before, her skin soft and glowing, her hair blonde and silky, her eyes sparkling with health. For an instant, Pandora thought she was looking at some newly arrived younger sister to her Great Aunt. Then she realised and could do nothing but stand and gape like a fish out of water.

Aunt Rachel laughed out loud, a rather unpleasant sound verging on hysteria. "Didn't I tell you?" she shrieked. "Lord, your face! I swear, you didn't recognise me for a moment!"

"I didn't," admitted Pandora frankly. "It's . . . just fantastic."

Aunt Rachel let her laughter subside. "Not really, my dear . . . though I suppose it might seem so to you. Here, come and sit down! I'm joining you for breakfast today and I think I may even manage *two* boiled eggs!"

"That's tremendous." Pandora sat beside her Great Aunt, noting as she did so that the woman's unpleasant body odour had vanished along with the lines and wrinkles. She wondered wryly if the mysterious age dissolving process included taking a bath.

"And how are you this morning?" asked Aunt Rachel.

"I'm fine, thanks."

"You hardly seem to be in the house at all lately. I wonder if we shouldn't keep you indoors for a few days. After all, we don't want you coming to grief in those woods. . . ."

"Oh, not in this lovely weather, surely," reasoned Pandora. "I'll be very careful."

"Well, we'll see." Myfanwy entered with the breakfast tray and served the meals. "Morning, love," she greeted Pandora. "I don't know if I'll see you tonight, before I leave. . . ."

"Leave?" cried Pandora.

"Well, of course. For the weekend. Cycle over to my sister's house in Brechfa, I do. I'll be back Sunday evening." With that, she breezed out of the room. Pandora felt decidedly apprehensive about it all. Somehow, Myfanwy was the one link with sanity in the entire household. The thought of two days alone with Ewen and Aunt Rachel was not a very cheerful prospect.

"Something wrong, Pandora?" Aunt Rachel's old, old eyes, in a strangely youthful face, studied her accusingly.

"No, no . . . I was . . . er, just wondering how we'll manage without her."

"Ewen does the cooking over the weekend. Actually, Myfanwy prepares the food beforehand; Ewen simply heats it up. You see, everything has been considered. We aren't expecting anything to go wrong." Aunt Rachel's words seemed oddly menacing.

They ate in silence. Pandora was hardly able to take her eyes from the little, silver charm hanging around the old woman's unwrinkled neck. It was the first time she had noticed it.

Myfanwy was right. It was exactly like the image in the sketchbook.

"Your move, Pandora!"

Pandora emerged from daydreams. "Sorry."

Aunt Rachel regarded her fixedly from the other side of the chessboard. "My goodness, you were miles away, young lady. Something on your mind?"

"No. Nothing." Pandora glanced down at the board. She was a poor chess player, always had been. She possessed the intelligent, logical mind needed to construct a plan of attack; but she was never able to focus her attention on the game long enough to see her ruse through. Now, she was hopelessly overrun, her knights and bishops lost and her king crouching abjectly in the midst of the confusion. "Just a matter of time now," she observed.

"Oh, yes," agreed Aunt Rachel. "A matter of time." She reached out and grasped Pandora's hand firmly. "Soon you'll be able to share my secret, too," she whispered. There was a kind of detached, faraway madness in her eyes now, that made Pandora look away quickly, afraid of what she saw in them. But the old woman crooned on, as though she hadn't noticed.

"Just think, my dear! Such a precious gift I'm going to give you. So priceless . . . why, all the wealth in the world couldn't purchase it." She gave a strange, little chuckle and then pointed back to the unfinished game. "Well, come along, Pandora. Let's get on with it, shall we?"

Pandora slid a pawn forward a space.

"This . . . secret, Aunt Rachel. You've never really explained much about it, have you? I mean, what *kind* of thing will it be?"

Aunt Rachel frowned. "You'll see, my dear. All in good time. Check!"

"Oh, dear . . . yes, but . . . surely you could tell me now. What difference can a day or two make?"

"All the difference in the world. You are too much like your namesake, Pandora. She was curious. Look what happened to her."

The door opened and Ewen stalked in. He hesitated by the entrance when he saw that Pandora was in the room. Aunt Rachel glanced at him coldly.

"Yes, Ewen?" she inquired.

"I've got the paints ready, Miss Ellis. And the canvas."

"Oh, good! There, Pandora, didn't I tell you that I'd be able to persuade Ewen to do your portrait?"

"Portrait?"

"Why, yes. Perhaps you'd like to sit for it this afternoon. Ewen's a very quick worker; it won't take more than a few hours. . . ."

"I can't, this afternoon. I have to go out."

"*Have* to, Pandora? You're not *meeting* somebody, by any chance?"

"No! No, it's just that it's a shame . . . to waste a lovely day like this. Perhaps, over the weekend. . . ."

"As you prefer. There's no immediate hurry, I suppose." She turned to Ewen. "Yes, I think *Sunday* will be ideal, Ewen." He nodded, went out again, closing the door behind him.

Aunt Rachel studied Pandora carefully. "You don't mind having a portrait done, do you?" she asked.

"No. Of course not."

"You're such a pretty child. I think we'll hang it over the fireplace, there. . . ."

"And take down the one that's there already?" cried Pandora. "What a shame to do that. That girl really *is* lovely."

"Yes," sighed Aunt Rachel. "So she was, so she was. But that's an old picture now, Pandora. The old must make way for the new, don't you think? Besides, it will be something to remember you by when you're gone."

"Gone?" whispered Pandora.

"Yes. Back to London."

"London. Oh, yes, London. Oh, I see. . . ." Almost with a sigh of relief, Pandora reached out and moved her king a square to the left. Aunt Rachel tutted softly. "Dear, dear Pandora, that *was* a silly thing to do. Now I shall have to make an end of you, once and for all." She slid her rook forward with an air of finality. "Checkmate!" she announced coldly. Then she reached out an exquisitely manicured finger and flipped Pandora's king off the board.

"The King is dead," she observed. "Long live the King!"

And she threw back her head and cackled, a long and hideous sound.

Chapter Eleven

Geraint was waiting in his usual place.

"You're late," he observed, a little testily, as Pandora approached.

"I'm sorry. I had a bit of trouble getting away." She regarded him for a moment, noticing the unfamiliar nervousness in his manner. Evidently, the experiences of the previous day were still heavy on his mind. He was carrying a hefty walking stick that would obviously double as a formidable weapon, should the necessity arise.

They stood for a moment in the middle of the road, uncertain of where to go. Neither of them felt inclined to wander into the green, waiting depths of the forest, that was for sure.

"Let's go up Bryn Myrrdin," suggested Geraint. He glanced quickly around. "At least it's open ground. . . ."

"Yes, all right."

They began to stroll along, side by side, deep in thought. The sunlight, streaming through the overhanging foliage, dappled their path with dancing shadows. In other times, under different circumstances, it would have been a day for laughter, for chasing each other across warm meadows, or simply lying in the grass, staring up at the vast, cloudless sky. Instead, they walked silently along, regarding their own footsteps, like two lost spectres beneath grey clouds of sorrow.

It was Geraint who spoke first.

"It really *did* happen, I suppose?" His voice was vague, tone-less. It was hardly a question at all.

"You know it happened."

"I . . . yes. I was wondering, that's all. If two people could have the same dream."

She shook her head. "Who are you trying to kid, Geraint? It was no dream. There was a place under the forest and a cave and a book. If you like, we'll go there again. . . ."

He grimaced. "That's all right, thankd You're right, of course; it really did happen. Thing is, what are we to do about it?"

They neared the edge of the wide meadow and made their way to the stile. Glancing back, Pandora suddenly became aware of Ewen, standing in the road some way behind them. He was studying them quite blatantly, his hands on his hips, a wisp of straw hanging from his mouth. It was obvious that he had fol-lowed them for a considerable distance.

"Well, of all the nerve!" exclaimed Pandora.

"What's the matter?" Geraint followed the direction of her gaze.

Ewen made no effort to pretend the situation was normal. He simply stood his ground and observed the two youngsters, a curi-ous smile on his face.

"That's torn it," muttered Pandora. "Come on, Geraint, let's get a move on." She clambered over the stile, virtually pulling her companion with her.

"Here, steady on, girl!" complained Geraint. "What's the hurry?"

"I just don't fancy hanging around in his company, that's all. You know, it wouldn't surprise me if Aunt Rachel sent him out to spy on us like that. She's been very suspicious lately and, for some reason, she has always warned me about talking to village children. . . . Ewen's bound to report back to her about it." She felt rather apprehensive about seeing Aunt Rachel again.

"I shouldn't worry, too much," advised Geraint. "After all, it's not as though she's your Mother. What can she say?"

Pandora shrugged. "Maybe you're right. . . . It's just a pity that she should find out *now*, when we're beginning to get some-where."

"I don't know about that," muttered Geraint gloomily. "I can't help thinking that we would do better to let well enough alone. After what happened yesterday . . . we nearly got caught."

Pandora fixed him with the familiar look of scorn.

"All that taught *me*," she said, "is to keep away from tunnels in future."

Geraint sighed. It was obvious that arguments were wasted on Pandora. The close call they'd had in the cave might have taken place years ago, for all the concern she showed. "Like water off a duck's back," he observed.

"What?"

"Nothing. Thinking aloud, I was. I suppose you want to go on snooping?"

"Of course. What else?"

"I don't know. . . . It's just . . . well, it's just that I've forgotten exactly what it is we're looking for, that's all. Everything has become so confused!"

"We're looking for the answers to questions, Geraint, as simple as that. For instance, you want to find out who your Father was, right?"

He nodded.

"And me, well, there's one hundred and one questions in my head and I know that the answers are all near at hand, if I only take the trouble to *look* for them. Which reminds me . . . is there any chance of getting hold of another torch?"

Geraint stopped in his tracks and stared at her.

"You're not thinking of. . . ."

"No!" exclaimed Pandora. "I'm not as reckless as all that, you know. This is for something else. The top floor of Savannah is all dark and boarded up and I need to have a look around."

Geraint shook his head. "I don't like the sound of that," he said.

"You don't have to like the sound of it! Can you get a torch or not?"

"I suppose so. When do you want it for?"

"The sooner, the better."

"Well, look . . . tomorrow's Saturday and I always help my Mother to do her shopping then; she likes me to stay home in the evening, too. . . . I don't expect I'll see you till Sunday afternoon. But if you like, I could come around late tonight and hide the torch in the grass, by the gates of the house."

"Oh, Geraint, would you? Myfanwy will be away over the weekend and I'll probably have a good chance of looking around. Aunt Rachel spends half her life in bed and Ewen's hardly ever about the place. . . ."

"Fair enough, then," said Geraint. "I'll hide it just to the right of the gates. I'll put it in a plastic bag, just in case it should rain. But for heaven's sake be careful with it, Pandora! How I shall explain losing the other one, I don't know. . . ."

"I'll be careful, all right. Don't worry." Pandora paused to lean upon a boulder for a moment. They had reached the base of the hill itself and the ground was getting steeper by the second. As usual, the crest of Bryn Myrrdin was cloaked by a low, brooding mist and it looked a long and arduous climb to the top. Pandora felt a great weariness bearing down on her.

"Let's not go any higher," she suggested. "I'm all in."

"I don't mind." Geraint sat himself down on a patch of thick, dry grass. Pandora flopped beside him with a sigh of contentment. She lay back, letting the sun warm her bones for a moment. She was suddenly aware that the meadow was alive with the singing of countless birds, the humming of a myriad unseen insects. It was funny how the mind could become so preoccupied with various problems, that such beauties could go completely unnoticed for a time. She felt the familiar warmth spreading within her, bringing with it the romantic sensation that she had first experienced the day she met Geraint. She reminded herself that while Bryn Myrrdin had introduced her to mystery and fear, it had also given her love. Once again, she found herself wary of that inadequate term. Trouble was, there didn't seem to be any alternative.

"Somebody should invent a new word for love," she sighed. "What do you think, Geraint?"

He made no reply. Glancing up, Pandora saw that he was gazing off into the distance, deep in thought. He obviously hadn't heard a word. The all too familiar troubled look was in his eyes. "The thing about Geraint," decided Pandora, "is that he *thinks* about things much more than he needs to. Sometimes it's better just to act on impulse. . . ." She reached out and placed her hand on his arm, squeezed it gently. He seemed to come out of his reverie and smiled at her.

"What's the trouble?" she asked him.

He shrugged. "Just worried, I suppose. . . ."

"About what?"

"About you. In that house. Pandora, I wish you would get out of there *now*, before something terrible happens. Even if it means you going back to London, I'd rather see that than . . . oh, I don't know. I've just got this feeling about the place. And you said yourself that your Aunt isn't worried what you find out. Aren't you afraid?"

"No," replied Pandora, and was absolutely amazed by the fact that she was telling the truth. "Isn't it funny, Geraint? I feel that I should be frightened and yet I'm not, really. It's almost as though, deep down, I keep telling myself that it's just a weird dream and it can't ever hurt me. When it really gets down to being hurtful, I'll wake up."

"But that's ridiculous! A moment ago you were saying. . . ."

"Yes, I know," interrupted Pandora. "But then, that's me. Changeable. But listen, Geraint, I've been waiting all my life for something like this to happen to me. Now it has, and whether it's a dream or whether it's real, I want to find out *everything*. You can understand that, can't you?"

"Yes. Yes, of course. . . . But not from a *girl!*" Pandora was abruptly reminded of the day that she first met Geraint; how he had been a little aloof at first, because of the superiority of his sex. She could see that it both bewildered and pleased him to find a girl who was so imbued with boyish qualities. In fact, of the two of them, she was the most headstrong, the most reckless. She had proved that much by taking the initiative in the exploration of the tunnel. Together they made an ideal team. Pandora's dash tempered by Geraint's cautiousness. Geraint's indecision galvanised by Pandora's fire. Take either one of them away and any chance of progress on the part of the remainder was doomed to failure.

Pandora frowned. "Geraint," she said. "When all this is over and I've gone back to London . . . will you write to me?"

He nodded vigourously. "Yes, of course. I'm not very good at letters, mind you, but I'll write just the same."

"Maybe one day you'll be able to come and visit me!"

"Wouldn't that be something, now! I've always wanted to see London."

Pandora warmed to her theme. "I could take you around the

sights . . . Piccadilly Circus . . . London Zoo . . . Madame Tussaud's . . . I know that we could put you up at the house for a while."

"Tremendous!"

They lay side by side in silence for a moment, their eyes mirrors of excitement. The sound of the birds seemed to fade away and the moment was trapped, timeless, like a jewelled butterfly beneath glass. Pandora was aware of a tense, thrilling excitement within her and, somehow, she was hardly able to breathe, such was the tightness in her breast. She *willed* Geraint to reach out and touch her and slowly, awkwardly, he did. He pushed close up against her, slid an arm around her neck and pulled her face close to his. Then his mouth was upon hers, pushing, probing, pressing down with increasing confidence. For a moment she panicked, recognising the urgent purpose in his advances. In the back of her mind a voice seemed to cry, "Is this love? Is this what people live for?" But then, abruptly the voice was gone, and she recognised the need in herself to search out the thing she had feared for so long and by finding it, destroy that fear forever.

They walked slowly across the meadow, arm in arm, in the last glow of afternoon. They hardly spoke to each other, both of them lost in secret thoughts.

Suddenly, they were no longer children and they were confused at how quick and easy the transformation had been. It had not been momentous in any way, just brief and fumbling and totally instinctive. And yet, there was a certain, all-pervading sadness about it, now that it was done.

Pandora felt two rivers of wetness trickle down her cheeks. She dashed them quickly away with her sleeve.

"Don't cry," whispered Geraint helplessly, thinking that she was full of remorse for what they had done.

He was wrong.

She was crying for all the summers to come, when she would search for the innocence she had once known and would never be able to find it.

Chapter Twelve

The gateway looked ominous in the failing light. Pandora and Geraint lingered by the entrance awhile, reluctant to part. It had turned chilly and Pandora shivered in her thin, cotton blouse. They were both at a loss for words.

After a few moments, Geraint kissed her gently on the lips and said,

"What time shall I meet you, Sunday?"

"In the morning . . . say, ten o'clock."

"Fine. Pandora . . . you're not angry, are you? About what happened. . . ."

She shook her head. "Of course not. I'm glad. I wanted you to." She glanced away to the dark, prying windows of the house. "I'd better go in now," she said. "I'm still a bit nervous about Ewen seeing us today. I'd like to get it over with."

"All right, then. See you Sunday."

"Oh, Geraint, that torch. . . ."

He grinned. "Don't worry, Sherlock Holmes! I haven't forgotten. Just you be careful, that's all." He pointed to a thick tuft of grass by the roadside. "I'll leave it right here," he added.

"Thanks. See you, then."

"Right."

They stood gazing at each other for a few moments longer, both of them wishing to stay awhile. Then, as if by mutual agreement, they turned away. Pandora moved slowly along the drive, her hands buried deep in the pockets of her jeans, her head bowed. The true meaning of her experience that afternoon was only beginning to dawn on her. She felt no shame or anything as silly as that, but there was a powerful, new quality within her that she was unable to define. It was as though she was subtly changed in body and mind; as though her very molecules had rearranged themselves to form a new Pandora. She was seeing the world through different eyes.

She let herself in through the back door, to find Myfanwy pottering about in the small parlour. She glanced up as Pandora entered.

"Ah, there you are now!" she exclaimed. "Getting worried, I was, thinking I would not see you before I left. . . . Why, whatever have you been up to, girl? Your hair is covered with grass!"

Pandora blushed involuntarily. Why was it that Myfanwy's every question seemed to touch upon one guilty secret or another?

"Here." Myfanwy handed Pandora a hairbrush. "I must say I cannot blame you at all. A lovely day it has been, for lying about in the meadows. If I were a few years younger and didn't have to work like I do, I daresay I'd be doing the same thing myself."

Now, Pandora had to smile, as she imagined stout old Myfanwy, lying in the long grass with some young fellow and . . . well, it didn't bear thinking about. She sat beside the fire and brushed her hair, keeping her smiling face turned away from Myfanwy's intuitive gaze.

"Aunt Rachel not about?" inquired Pandora at length.

"I'm afraid she went to her room early. Your own entertainment you must make tonight, I think. . . ."

"That's all right." Pandora tried not to sound relieved. "How will you get to Brechfa, Myfanwy?"

"I have an old bicycle in the garage."

"Golly. I must say I don't envy you riding along that road in the dark."

Myfanwy chuckled. "Why, bless you, lights I have got. . . . Though I suppose I know what you mean. A bit creepy it is, with all those trees on either side . . . mind you, once you have been along it as often as I have, you wouldn't give it a second thought."

"Have you ever seen a ghost on the road?" asked Pandora.

"A ghost. . . ?" Myfanwy seemed undecided about how best to answer that.

"A little boy with no clothes on," prompted Pandora.

"Well . . . yes, yes I have! Not sure, I was, whether to say yes or no, in case it might frighten you. But I suppose you must have seen it, too."

Pandora nodded. "In the garden," she replied. "Twice."

"There now! What can I say? A ghost there is all right, but not one as would hurt anybody, of that I am sure. Sometimes, when I am riding home, he passes by me along the road. He never says anything, just stares at me with those empty eyes of his. Mind you, the first time I ever saw him I near fell off my bike, I was so frightened! Just a poor lost soul he is and nothing for you to worry about."

"Oh, I'm not worried. I just wondered if you knew anything about him. Who he was before, I mean."

Myfanwy turned away suddenly and Pandora thought she saw a troubled glint in the woman's eyes.

"I wouldn't know, miss," she answered sharply. Then, she turned back and said in a more gentle voice, "It's *all right*, Pandora, nothing's going to happen. I'll look after you. I'll be back on Sunday evening, so just be careful. . . ." She seemed to think better of what she was saying and made an exaggerated display of looking at her wristwatch. "Goodness, is that the time?" she cried. "I'll have to get a move on!"

"Myfanwy, what did you mean about being careful?"

"Oh, nothing, I just . . . don't go running into any trees, that is all." She bustled about sorting out her bits and pieces.

"Shall I fetch your bike?" suggested Pandora.

"Oh, would you, love? That would be a help."

Obediently, Pandora slipped through the kitchen and out of the back door. It was now quite dark and very cold. She found the garage doors open and, flicking on the light, she went inside. Myfanwy's bike, an ancient pile of black, rusting metal, was leaned up against Ewen's station waggon. As Pandora leaned over to take the handlebars, something inside the car caught her attention. On the dashboard, by the driver's seat, rested a small, familiar lilac-coloured envelope. It was addressed to her, in her Mother's elegant handwriting.

"What?" she exclaimed, mystified. She had hardly expected a reply to her letter so soon, for she knew that the speed of any communication depended entirely upon when Ewen decided to drive into Brechfa to collect the mail. Without hesitation, she tested the door handle and found to her relief that it was unlocked. Reaching in, she grabbed the envelope and examined it briefly. She felt a shock of pure anger when she realised that the letter had been opened. The envelope was daubed with grubby fingerprints.

"Ewen!" she whispered hoarsely "Of all tho norvo. . . ." Fuming, oho thrust the letter into her back pocket and wheeled the rickety bike outside. Myfanwy was waiting by the back door, wrapped in a huge grey overcoat.

"Thank you, love," she said.

Pandora watched silently as Myfanwy eased her bulk onto the saddle.

"Mind how you go," she advised.

"I will, Pandora. See you Sunday!"

And with that she creaked unsteadily away, along the drive, into the darkness. Pandora watched until she was out of sight and then hurried inside. The house seemed horribly empty. Forsaking the warmth of the fire, she went straight upstairs to her bedroom, closed the door carefully and, sitting down on the bed, took out the letter.

She read through it quickly.

My dearest Pandora.

I bet you didn't expect to hear from me so soon, did you darling! The fact is that I hurried straight home from the station the day you left and burst into tears. I think your Father thought I had gone loopy or something! Anyway, here it is only Wednesday and even though I'm sure you've already written and that the letters will cross, I simply had to write to you and let you know that I miss you terribly. (John does too, though of course, he would never admit to anything so human!)

We are both working like mad at doing absolutely nothing and we haven't had a single row in three days, which I feel must be some kind of record. Gerry Michaels came around today; you remember, the fat bald-headed gentleman from the film company who calls you "freckles"! He brought with him a film script and an offer to work with one of Britain's top directors. I simply said "no" and I can honestly say that it was the most exhilarating experience of my life. Poor Gerry . . . at first he thought I was joking. When he realised I wasn't, he simply exploded. (I'm glad you weren't there to hear the language!)

John has really been trying, too. He's locked the door to his study and intends to do no writing whatsoever for at least six months. It's all going so well and the only thing missing is *you*, Pandora. I know how you feel about all this, love, and you've been an angel, but please come back to us soon. I've included a note for Aunt Rachel, saying that as soon as you feel ready, she's to put you on the next train for Paddington, where we'll be waiting with open arms. Of course, if you are having a good time in Wales and you want to stay on awhile, then that's completely up to you. I'd just hate to think that you're sticking with it because of us.

Well, that's all for now. Write to us soon (if you haven't already; and if not, why not)? All my love, darling, and even a kiss from your Father. He *must* be missing you!

Love,
Sammy.

The note intended for Aunt Rachel was missing.

Frowning, Pandora laid the letter down on the bed. Why had it been opened without her knowledge? And why had it been kept from her? Any amateur detective would know how to steam open a letter, read the contents and then pass it on again, without leaving any visible trace of the intrusion. But this envelope had been roughly torn by someone who had no intention of letting it go further. What was in the letter that Ewen or Aunt Rachel was reluctant to let Pandora see? The invitation to go home again?

"They want to keep me here," she thought to herself. "Not because they *like* me or anything. . . . There's some other reason."

She glanced at the envelope again, noting the black fingerprints that were smeared across her Mother's delicate writing. If she hadn't gone into the garage by sheer chance, then she never would have learned of the letter's existence. Her anger deepened. Whatever the reasons for this, it was about time she found out for herself. She would go to Aunt Rachel's room and hammer on the door, demand to know what it was all about.

Without hesitation, she got up and went out of her room, then strode along the dimly-lit landing, to Aunt Rachel's door. She lifted her hand to knock . . . then stopped.

Voices. Inside the room. A man and a woman. She concentrated for a moment and recognised Ewen's gruff tones and Aunt Rachel's easy drawl. But what were they saying? Involuntarily, she moved her head close to the door and listened intently. Then, on second thought, she kneeled down and peered through the keyhole. The room was dimly lit by a small bedside lamp and she could make out the figure of Aunt Rachel, sitting up in bed. Ewen was out of her vision but occasionally his shadow passed in front of the keyhole, as though he was pacing up and down the room.

He was talking heatedly. Pandora concentrated.

". . . I tell you. I saw them together on the road, walking. He's one of my brats, all right, I'd recognise him anywhere. . . ."

Aunt Rachel chuckled. "You should be more careful with your wild oats, Ewen. How did this particular 'brat' come into existence?"

"Some woman in the village . . . I was taken with her looks. A long time ago, now, maybe ten, fifteen years. . . ."

"And no bedroom is safe from the Lord of the Incubus, eh? At least, that was the case, *then*. But I think we've quite broken your spirit now, haven't we, Ewen? Any freedom I feel inclined to give you and you just run hell for leather to your home, yelling like a wounded bobcat! What do you *do* there Ewen?"

"I live."

"Incubus," echoed Pandora thoughtfully. Geraint had told her about that. And it was obvious now that Ewen really was Geraint's Father. Aunt Rachel spoke again.

"There will be no more freedom for a while, Ewen. Not until the three days are up at any rate. I don't want any repetition of what happened the other day. . . ."

"I've told you, there's no chance of that! I've put a new watcher at the gate. I've applied more preparation and gone right through the ritual again. It's just that the last carcass had fallen off, that's all. . . ."

"How could it have?"

"Flesh rots. It's as simple as that."

"You're supposed to keep check on the damned thing! Remember, this is the *third* time it's happened, now."

"I do check. Maybe it's *her* making it fall."

A look of fear came into the old woman's eyes.

"Is that possible?"

"Perhaps. Her will to escape is stronger now than it's ever been. She seems to sense that the time is close. . . ."

"Well, I'm taking no more chances! I called you and you sure as hell took your time getting back. I very nearly died. . . ."

"Nearly."

Aunt Rachel threw back her head and cackled. "Oh, you'd dearly love that, wouldn't you! But it isn't going to happen, not so long as I have the charm . . . and that'll be a good long time yet. At least another sixty years!"

"Haven't you done enough living, Rachel?" cried Ewen. "How can you be greedy for another sixty years? You've had your time."

"Maybe." Aunt Rachel nodded slowly. "Maybe I have, at that. But you're forgetting, Mr. Incubus, you're forgetting that I was only a young girl when I began it. I've really only had the benefit of the last twenty years or so; and there's *nothing* to say that I can't do it all over again! Nothing's going to stop me from looking young and pretty, not if I have to do it over and over. . . ."

There was a long pause. Then Ewen spoke again, slowly and carefully, in a voice that was loaded with contempt.

"You talk about beauty," he said, "and you are the ugliest woman I have ever known. Your face is lined with deceit. Your skin is transparent and inside, you are heavy with your sins. I have to play this game. For me there has never been any choice, not so long as the charm is yours. You have always been aware of the evil of this process, the evil that drove many people to madness before you were even born. Your Uncle Alex knew what he was doing when he left the charm to you, Rachel. He recognised in you a loathsome quality that few people are ever cursed with. Over the years, I have watched your ugliness grow, reminding myself occasionally that you are supposed to be a human being. Your soul, if you have one, must be as black as hell itself."

Aunt Rachel stared at him for several moments, lost in thought. Then she brought her hands together in a burst of mocking applause.

"A beautiful little speech Ewen!" she cried. "And so appropriate from one as pure as yourself."

"I have never pretended to be pure!"

"Quite so, Ewen, quite so! What about the child, eh? You want her, don't you? I've seen you watching her. . . . I know how you think. Wouldn't you just love to take her? Well, wouldn't you?"

"Be quiet! All men are prisoners of their own weakness. . . ."

"And none more so than you, dear little incubus! Ironic, isn't it? How you must long for her innocence . . . how you must dream of taking it from her. . . . Well, you know something, Ewen, I just might let you do it! I might let you at that, provided you're a good boy, of course."

"Stop it! For the love of. . . ."

"God, Ewen? You can't ask him for help, now can you? Neither of us can do that." She reached up a hand and fingered the silver charm around her neck casually. "But never mind, my dear," she crooned softly. "I understand. I'll give you what you want . . . but first you must earn it." She gave the silver charm a squeeze. "And right now, it's *me* you want. Isn't that right?"

A kind of strangled moan was his only reply.

"Come here," commanded Aunt Rachel coldly. The charm in her fingers seemed to glitter with an unnatural light. Again, she tightened her grasp upon it.

Pandora could only peer in horrified fascination as he stumbled into sight, moving like a man in a daze, towards the old woman's bed. His head was turned away but, somehow, Pandora could sense the look of revulsion upon his face. Aunt Rachel let the blankets drop from her body and she lay back against her pillows, laughing derisively as Ewen reached out to her with shaking hands. . . .

"Oh, lord," whispered Pandora. "Oh, lord, oh no, no, no!"

For she was watching the very thing that she and Geraint had done, only that very afternoon. But it had changed horribly.

What had seemed a joyful, loving, sharing experience had become a writhing, degrading dance of corruption. The two groping figures on the bed had only one thing in common; mutual loathing.

Sobbing with revulsion, Pandora fell away from the door and lay for a moment on the cold floor, shaking her head slowly from side to side. It had not seemed like that with Geraint. Supposing, one day, she would become that empty? Was that what had happened to her parents? Was that what happened to everyone? Her eyes filled with tears. She did not want to believe it.

Quickly, she got up and ran to the dark seclusion of her bedroom.

It was very late. Pandora lay awake, her mind a rippled pool of confusion. She was not sure what she had learned from the conversation. Ewen was Geraint's Father, that much was certain. But what of the other things she'd heard? It seemed that Ewen was somehow a slave to Aunt Rachel and that the silver Goblin charm was the key to this. The really puzzling thing had been the repeated mention of "sixty years" and also, Aunt Rachel's statement about Ewen's longing for "the child." Pandora knew with a dread conviction that this could only refer to herself.

She was sure that Geraint was talking good sense, when he advised her to leave the house quickly; and yet, even now, some submerged part of her unconscious mind urged her to go on with the quest, to seek and discover the final secret. It was as though her mind was no longer her own, as though it had become a harbour for lost souls who were gently, insistently guiding her along a vague, ill-defined path.

"What's the matter with me?" she asked herself weakly. "I *want* to go. I'm frightened to stay here any longer. . . ." It would be so easy to do. She had enough money, she could sneak out tomorrow and find her way to Carmarthen and the station . . . but then a voice inside her said, "No, you must stay! Think of the *other* children!" This voice did not seem to be her own. She wondered vaguely if she was going insane.

"What other children?" she asked the voice in her head. And the answer came back, as though from the shores of a far-off land. "You will see. Stay. Search. Then you will understand."

She had never felt so small and lost in her entire life.

Night winds went sighing past her window. She glanced at her wristwatch. One A.M., just gone. She stiffened slightly at the sound of her door opening. She lay unmoving, her eyes half closed in imitation of sleep. Her heart pounded fearfully within her. Whoever it was waited on the edge of her vision for several long moments, breathing softly, as though unsure of what to do. Then from out of the darkness, a figure approached.

Pandora felt an electric jolt of fear slam into her as, through the fuzzy windows of her drooping eyelashes, she recognised Ewen, standing over her and looking down with his familiar, impassive stare. Aunt Rachel's words seemed to echo through Pandora's head.

"What about the child, eh? You want her, don't you? I've seen you watching her. . . . I know how you think. Wouldn't you just love to take her? Well, wouldn't you?"

"Oh, no!" thought Pandora desperately. "Please God, no, don't let him."

Ewen seemed to stand there for an eternity. Then suddenly, he reached out a hand towards Pandora's face. She tensed herself, preparing to give a scream that would raise the roof. But she never uttered it. Ewen's hand came to rest upon her head. He gave her hair a gentle, almost tender stroke and leaning forward, touched his lips softly against her cheek.

Pandora lay there stunned and amazed.

A beam of moonlight from the window had caught and illuminated his eyes; there was a deep, lost sadness in them and they were brimming with tears. She felt a twinge of compassion rise within her, but still she feigned sleep, afraid of what he might do if she reacted to him. He drew back from the bed a little, never taking his eyes off her. Then silently he turned and walked back to the door. Pandora let out a soft sigh of relief. She waited for the creak of door hinges but it never came. Instead, there was the abrupt click of a key turning in a lock.

Almost instantly he was back, leaning forward over the bed. Again his face was illuminated by the moonlight, but now it had changed horribly. Every shred of compassion had disappeared from it. It was the gaunt, leering mask of a depraved animal.

Pandora opened her mouth to scream, but then a powerful hand was clamped over her jaw, while another dragged her blankets aside, began to tear at her cotton nightdress, in an impatient frenzy. She tried desperately to kick and struggle but she was held like a doll in his powerful grasp and she could only lie in horrified submission as his free hand caressed her, his sharp fingernails clawing at her flesh. A great, silent scream welled up inside her, until it seemed to shake her body with its confined power.

And then he was on top of her, not gentle like Geraint, but savage and powerful, strong enough to crush her like a toy, if he so desired. She could not take her gaze from his eyes. In the darkened room, they seemed to burn before her vision, like two spheres of flame.

Abruptly, her fear melted away and was replaced by a strange, exhilarating sensation, deep inside. His hand was gone from her mouth. She noticed this almost absent-mindedly. She could scream now . . . she could scream for help and perhaps somewhere, somebody might hear her, send help. . . .

Instead, she lifted her head, until her eyes were mere inches away from Ewen's gaze and then she smiled strangely and pressed her lips against his. Then she just lay back, aware of desire flooding through her body and wishing vaguely that it might go on forever.

Chapter Thirteen

Pandora stepped out of the front door, into the cold embrace of morning. It was barely seven o'clock and everything was grey and misty. She had hardly slept at all after Ewen had gone, assailed by fears and doubts and those insistent voices which were gradually assuming characters of their own. They had pleaded with her, cajoled her, begged her with single-minded purpose to stay in the house until the mystery was solved. At one point, just before the dawn, the voices had seemed to emerge from her head and fill the house with their crazy whisperings, until she had been forced to sit up in her bed and cry out, "Who are you?"

"The children," had returned the answer, in a long, sighing chorus that ran through the ancient, timbered house, like water along a dry river bed. And then, they were gone and she heard them no more.

Now, here she stood, on the steps of Savannah, and all thought of running away had indeed been banished from her mind. She breathed the chill air deep into her lungs for a moment, then descended the steps and walked slowly along the drive, the loose gravel crunching beneath her feet. At the gates, she paused for a moment, not wanting to be observed. She glanced around. There was not a soul in sight.

She bent over and examined the grass to the right of the entrance. She found the cellophane-wrapped object exactly where Geraint had said it would be, half hidden in a thick clump of grass. The thought of him caused her a sudden twinge of guilt. Whatever would he think if he were to learn of her latest experience? It was as though she had aged ten years since she last saw him. She still didn't quite understand what had happened to her the previous evening. How could she have *enjoyed* such an ordeal? The memory of it seemed to fill her with a curious mingling of shame and excitement. For the first time in her life, she was frightened by her own intentions. She sighed, frowned, reached down to pick up the torch.

"What are you looking for?" The loud voice made her spin around, a look of guilt on her face.

Ewen was standing in the middle of the drive, only a few feet away from her.

"Where on earth did you come from?" exclaimed Pandora helplessly.

He declined to answer that. He simply stood looking at her in silent accusation, his hands thrust casually into the pockets of his jeans. His face bore the same expression of detached indifference that it had as he left the bedroom earlier that morning. He had not even spoken a word to her, but had simply stood up, rearranged his clothing, and left. Again, he repeated his question.

"What are you looking for?"

"I . . . I was . . . picking flowers," stammered Pandora. It was a miserable lie. The grass on which she stood was completely devoid of any kind of bloom. Ewen's gaze flicked rapidly across the stretch of ground, as though evaluating the plausibility of her story. Perhaps his eyes registered the incriminating parcel that lay half in, half out of shadow; perhaps he saw nothing. He frowned, looked away to the distant trees, a curious longing in his eyes.

"His home," thought Pandora suddenly. "Where he wants to be, right now. . . . Why doesn't he just go there?"

"You're up early," observed Ewen, after a lengthy pause.

"Yes. . . ." She stood her ground awkwardly, not sure of what to say, but knowing that Ewen was not one to make idle conversation. "It's good to be up early once in a while. . . . The air tastes so clean."

"Does it?" He stared at her curiously for a moment and then

his expression seemed to soften abruptly, his lips curving into the vaguest ghost of a smile. He took a long deep breath himself and nodded. "You're right," he admitted lamely. "It does."

Pandora felt much cheered by this small admission of humanity. She reminded herself that this was the same man who had assaulted her only a few hours ago, bringing her pain and humiliation . . . and more besides, a strange, gnawing hunger deep inside, that she never dreamed could ever exist. She sensed a new attitude within him now, an altogether more approachable side to his character, that seemed to be fighting a battle with his other self. Ewen opened his mouth to speak again, but oddly, no sound escaped from his lips. He grimaced, closed his eyes, as though making the greatest effort to find words.

"What's the matter?" prompted Pandora.

He shook his head, shrugged, seeming to think better of his actions. Once again, the look of indifference masked his face. He turned away and began to walk towards the house, his head down.

Pandora stared after him, wondering what was wrong. An impulse made her shout after him.

"Wait! Ewen, do you hate me?"

He paused for a moment, then turned back.

"No," he replied. "I don't hate *you*. Only what you mean to me."

"And what's that?"

"Sixty years," he muttered. "Another sixty years. . . ."

"But I don't understand. Can't you explain?"

"It's not for me to explain to you. My task is to help *her*. That's all I know. Believe me, if I could help you in any way, I would. . . . What happened last night . . . it was. . . ." Once again, he seemed unable to explain himself. He turned away and plodded along the drive and around the back of the house, out of sight.

Pandora sighed and bent to retrieve the torch. She slipped it into her back pocket and she, too, began to stroll in the direction of Savannah. It was funny how Ewen had appeared like he did, so suddenly, apparently out of thin air. And strange, too, how he had tried to say something and had been unable to. What had he been attempting to tell her? And who had stopped him? Aunt Rachel, back in the coldness of her bedroom? Pandora imagined the young-old woman, crouched in a dark corner like a demented puppeteer, pulling on a web of invisible strings that would make Ewen dance to her every tune.

She went around to the back of the house and let herself in. The kitchen looked awfully bare without Myfanwy bustling about the place and the small parlour was even less cheerful. She climbed quietly up the staircase and hid the torch in her bedroom. All being well, she would conduct her little search that evening. She realised that her Mother's letter was still lying on the floor and she hid that away, too, in one of the drawers of the dressing table. Then she threw open the window and sat down on the bed, in order to watch the morning metamorphose into day.

Her mind was a nest of confusion and, for the moment at least, she didn't want to think any more than she had to.

At about nine o'clock there was a soft rapping at the door.

"Come in," called Pandora, knowing that it could only be one of two people. The door opened and Aunt Rachel padded into the room.

"Ah, good morning, my dear. Up with the lark, I see."

Pandora hoped that her increasing dislike for the old woman did not show on her face. She found herself unable to look into those searching eyes, for the memories of the previous night were still powerful on her mind.

"Good morning, Aunt Rachel," she replied tonelessly, turning her gaze back to the window. "How are you today?"

"Just dandy! Fresh as a daisy, in fact!" She moved over to the bed and peered over Pandora's shoulder. "Fine morning," she enthused. "It's going to be a beautiful day. What say we go down and have a little breakfast?"

"I'm really not very hungry."

"Nonsense, girl. We've got to keep you in trim. . . . Whatever would your Mother say if she thought I wasn't feeding you?" She peered at Pandora intently. "Now you *are* looking a tiny bit pale this morning," she said. "But all the more reason for getting a good meal inside you. Come along now, I'll get Ewen to fix us something. . . ."

Suddenly, Pandora couldn't bear to see Ewen made to do anything of the sort.

"Let me do it," she suggested. "I feel like making myself useful for a change. That will be all right, won't it?"

Aunt Rachel shrugged.

"Just as you wish, my dear. Just as you wish."

She led the way out of the room and down the stairs. She still carried her walking stick, but Pandora could see that she hardly put any weight upon it. She seemed to be using it merely from force of habit. She remembered back, only a few days, to when Myfanwy and she had struggled to carry Aunt Rachel up that same staircase, an Aunt Rachel of a far different appearance to the one who now strolled so easily along. Pandora wondered if that was what she had been referring to in the conversation with Ewen, when she said that she had almost died.

They reached the kitchen and Pandora set about preparing the old woman's customary boiled egg, while Aunt Rachel set the table in the dining room. Pandora herself could stomach nothing more substantial than a bowl of corn flakes. They ate together in silence and then, at Aunt Rachel's suggestion, adjourned to the sitting room for a game of chess. Pandora went through the motions with a kind of weary resignation, but her thoughts were elsewhere.

There was in her mind the most vivid recollection of Ewen's blazing eyes, staring down at her from the darkness of her bedroom. His hands clawing and tearing at her skin. His mouth, hard and cruel, clamped like a vise against her own eager lips. . . .

Her head seemed to reel with a multitude of forbidden images. She closed her eyes, thinking she might faint.

"Pandora," said Aunt Rachel unexpectedly. "I don't know where your thoughts are today, but they certainly aren't on this game of chess. You've just put yourself right into check."

"Oh, I'm sorry. . . . I'm afraid I'm not quite with it today."

Aunt Rachel leaned back in her chair and studied Pandora thoughtfully, one hand fidgeting absent-mindedly with the charm around her neck. Pandora was unable to take her eyes from the tiny silver figure as it turned around and around between the woman's slim fingers. She recalled how Aunt Rachel had done just the same action on the previous night, as she compelled poor Ewen to walk across the room, to reach out for her body, to. . . .

Again, Pandora closed her eyes, trying desperately to blot out the scene that haunted her mind so vividly. She was sure that it would be her waking nightmare for many weeks to come.

"Is something troubling you, Pandora?" asked Aunt Rachel quietly. She sounded genuinely concerned.

"No. . . ." whispered Pandora. "No . . . nothing. . . ." Then, with a sudden dash of bravado, she added, "I just wish Mummy would write me a letter, that's all. She promised me she'd send one, the very first chance she got."

Aunt Rachel didn't bat an eyelid.

"I'm sure she will soon, Pandora. You must remember that the postal service here is very bad. Ewen hasn't had a chance to get into the village lately either; who knows, there might be one waiting at the post office at this very minute."

"Liar!" thought Pandora bitterly. It took a powerful effort not to give vent to her feelings. "When *will* Ewen be going into Brechfa?" she asked.

"Well . . . certainly not today, my dear, he has far too much work. Perhaps early next week." She switched the subject. "Don't forget that you're having your portrait done tomorrow, Pandora. It's really quite an honour, you know! I bet you're pretty thrilled about it all, aren't you?"

"Oh, yes," murmured Pandora unconvincingly. "Thrilled."

"And, of course, it's *all* tied in with our little secret!"

"Secret?"

"You remember! We were talking about it only the other day . . . my secret of youth. Well, in a few days' time, I'll be ready to let you in on the whole caboodle. . . ."

Pandora felt distinctly uneasy.

"Aunt Rachel, I'm really not sure about all this," she announced. "I mean, I've been thinking about it a lot. It's really nice of you and everything, but I don't know if I *want* to share anything like that. . . ."

"What?" Aunt Rachel looked positively outraged. "But that's nonsense, my girl, absolute nonsense. Do you realise how much of an honour this is? Why, I very nearly chose another little girl to give the gift to. A little girl from the village, she was, not even related to me. It was all planned that it would be her and then I got your Father's letter and naturally I changed those plans without a moment's thought! I never *dreamed* that you would be so ungrateful. . . ."

"It's not that I'm ungrateful," reasoned Pandora. "It's just that I don't have any idea what it's all about and I'm afraid. . . ."

"Afraid?" cried Aunt Rachel. "Of me? How can you possibly say that, child? What reason have I given you to be afraid of me?"

"Well, no, I didn't mean . . . I just . . . just. . . ." Pandora bowed her head in defeat. She couldn't say how she really felt about her Great Aunt and the big, frightening house in which she lived. She had to play the game cautiously, go along with her Aunt's intrigues all the way. Then she would see what was really happening here. "I'm sorry. . . ." she muttered lamely.

"There, there," crooned Aunt Rachel sympathetically. She reached out and took Pandora's hands in her own, which were as cold and uninviting as a block of ice. "You're not to worry about a thing now, Pandora. After all, you know that I'm your friend and I wouldn't dream of upsetting you. Just wait and see what my secret is! You *do* want to share it with me, don't you?"

"Yes," said Pandora tiredly. "Yes, of course. . . ."

Aunt Rachel chuckled softly. She released Pandora's hands and, leaning back in her chair, she surveyed the chessboard for a moment.

"Well, now. It's still your move," she said.

Pandora lay on the bed, fully clothed.

The last soft movements in the house had ended nearly an hour ago. The time was a little after twelve o'clock. She decided to wait just a few moments longer, to allow Aunt Rachel time to sink deeper into dreams.

The day had been interminable, long and suffocating in its isolation. Aunt Rachel was hideous company. She had insisted on babbling on about her wretched secret, until Pandora could have quite cheerfully strangled her. Ewen had made a brief appearance in the afternoon to serve a late dinner and then, just as promptly, had gone missing again. Pandora hadn't felt too hungry, but had managed to force some of the meal down in order to stop the old woman going on about "keeping up strength" and the like. She had retired as early as was politely possible. And she had waited for nightfall and the chance to seek some answers to questions she hadn't dared to ask.

The whispering voices had begun again; she could hear them quite distinctly, tiny insect buzzings in the back of her mind. "Now!" they urged her. "Look, look upstairs. . . ."

Still, she resisted the impulse to rise awhile longer. She lay still, the cold metal torch gripped in her hand, her eyes staring out into the unlit room. She felt terribly uneasy about the whole venture, now that she was faced with it. She remembered how confident she'd been, leading the way down the tunnel beneath the forest earth. Supposing the boarded-up top floor held similar horrors in its dark, slumbering rooms? She shivered uncontrollably for a moment, then steeled herself with an effort.

"Now!" cried the voices in unison. "Go now! Hurry!"

Softly, she got up off the bed. She crossed the room and gently opened the door. She peered out into blackness. Flicking on the torch, she let the bright beam explore every inch of the landing before she allowed herself to take another step. The stair rails looked gaunt and evil in the glow; beyond them, the deep steps waited like a black pit. Cautiously, Pandora began to move along the landing, putting her feet down with excruciating care. The slightest creak seemed to echo in the unreal vacuum in which she moved. She drew level with Aunt Rachel's door, half expecting it to crash open and reveal her Great Aunt's vengeful figure. Nothing happened. She moved on, past the bathroom and along, her heart pounding like a great hammer in her chest. All too soon, she reached the end of the landing.

Now, before her, was the old rickety staircase, mildewed and rotten with age. She hesitated for a few seconds. The voices in her head seemed to rise to a shrill frenetic crescendo and she was unable to think now. She reached out a hand and gripped the bannister rail, then placed a foot carefully on the first step.

The voices were gone!

Abruptly, she was free of them. She stood there at the foot of the stairs in shocked surprise. Why had they ceased? The torch illuminated the rough wooden screen before her. Determinedly, she eased her way up to it, only too aware of the noise her progress made. After a few moments she stood beside it. She took hold of the hinged section and swung it back. Once again, that icy blast of air tore at her face. Once again, she was struck by the horrible stench of mould and rot. She very nearly turned back at that instant; but something made her push through the opening with the torch light blazing before her.

The wooden pendulum swung back behind her.

The landing was much like the one below, except that it was dirty and festooned with curtains of cobweb and patches of fungus. Searching around, Pandora found a light switch on the wall. She reached up and flicked it on. Miraculously, the lights still worked and the place looked far less threatening in the realistic glow of electric light. Slipping the torch into her pocket, Pandora approached the closed door of the first room. She tested the handle carefully and it opened into darkness. She found a light switch just within and tried it. No luck. She took out her torch again and stepped inside. It was devoid of any furniture whatsoever. The only thing of any interest was a large painting stacked against the far wall. She went over to it and saw that it was so obscured by dust that the image was lost. She wiped at it with her sleeve for a moment and shone the beam onto it again. She gasped.

It was a portrait of a young boy, a boy she recognised instantly. Though she had only seen him three times in her life, she could never mistake that pale, staring face. It was the ghost boy. He was dressed in a strange suit of clothes and a flat, cloth cap. The date in the corner of the portrait was 1909; it had the same indecipherable autograph as the painting of the little girl in Aunt Rachel's front room.

Pandora frowned. "Another Ewen original?" she wondered. What was it all about? She thought of Aunt Rachel's eagerness for the latest portrait and she felt cold inside. Would such a happening leave Pandora dead and white, to wander the dark gardens of the world forever?

She stepped back from the painting and her foot clumped against wood with a noise that seemed to reverberate through the entire house. Her heart in her mouth, she turned and in the glare of the torch, she saw a small, open coffin lying on the dusty floor. She stifled an exclamation of surprise and tried to reassure herself that as long as it was empty, there was nothing to fear. She kneeled beside it and saw that it was half full with a greasy mixture of mud and what looked like chopped leaves. It was giving off a disgusting, powerful, yeasty odour. She stood up quickly, not wanting to inquire too closely into the measurements of the thing. Numbly, she turned away from the coffin and came out onto the landing again. The next door was very interesting. This one, she guessed, must have been directly over the bathroom on the next floor. The door was a huge, oaken affair, studded with points of black, tarnished metal. As Pandora approached it, she could see that something was fixed onto it, a strange, hunched shape, black and furry. Puzzled, she stepped closer; then, she had to suppress a scream of revulsion as she realised what it was. A wave of nausea flooded her stomach.

It was the bloodstained body of a cat, impaled against the wood by a huge nail, driven into its left eye and through the back of its skull. Judging by the contortion of its limbs and tail, the act had been performed while the creature was still alive. Pandora remembered the brief, wailing scream she had heard a couple of days ago and, more recently, Ewen's mention of a "watcher at the gate." Her blood seemed to freeze within her veins. She could see several holes in the door, where other nails had been driven in the past, and the ancient wood was stained dark with long congealed blood. Trying hard not to allow her gaze to focus on the dead animal, Pandora forced herself to examine the door more closely.

It looked as though it had not been opened in years, because the edges of it were sealed tight with an evil-looking black glue. Pandora chipped at some of this with her fingernail and a small piece flaked off into her hand. She sniffed at it and noticed that it had a powerful, herbal smell that was rather unpleasant. Then she took hold of the door handle and gave it an exploratory twist.

"Who's there?"

Pandora stiffened. The voice had come from within the room. She had never dreamed that anyone might be up there in the darkness. She considered whether or not to run away. The voice came again, nearer to the door this time, the small, unfamiliar sound of a young girl.

"Please, whoever it is, don't go!"

Silence for a moment. Pandora's mind raced. What would anybody be doing up in this dismal place at such a late hour?

Again the voice.

"Listen, I know there's somebody there. Is it the little girl, the one I've seen walking in the garden? Please answer. . . ."

"My . . . my name's Pandora. . . ."

"Pandora! That's a lovely name. My name is Ellen. Ellen Hughes."

Pandora pressed closer to the door.

"Look, I'm sorry, I don't understand. Shall I open the door for you?"

"You can't. It's locked."

"Well, who's got the key, then?"

"*She* has, the old witch! She keeps me locked up here all the time. I've been trying to signal to you, now and again. Have you heard me, banging on the floor?"

"Yes . . . yes, I have . . . but listen, you say *she* keeps you in there. Do you mean Aunt Rachel?"

"I don't know her name. The woman who runs the place. She's had me in here for as long as I can remember, now."

"But why?"

A long, drawn-out sigh from beyond the door.

"I don't know. . . . What does it matter, anyway. She does it. . . . Pandora, you must help me to get out of here!" The voice seemed tinged with desperation.

"Of course," replied Pandora, wishing vainly that she could see the girl's face. "Of course I'll help. Tomorrow I'll go to the police station in the village. I'll fetch somebody here. Whatever it is you've done, they'll get you out. . . ."

"No, no, no! That's no good at all. We need the key! It has to be the key. . . . The old woman will have it somewhere, hidden away. Find that and bring it up here. Once I'm out, there's nothing to worry about."

Pandora scratched her head.

"Look, I don't get this at all. If Aunt Rachel has locked you up for some reason, then she should be punished for it, surely. The police will do that. . . ."

"She'll be punished all right. But not by the police. Trust me, Pandora, I've had plenty of time to think about this over the years."

"Over the *years?* Ellen, how old are you?"

"Never mind that! Listen carefully. There isn't much time left,

I know. A few days, perhaps, and neither of us will have a chance. Have they painted a picture of you, yet?"

"A picture . . . no, that's supposed to happen tomorrow."

"Don't let it happen! Fight if you have to! I let them paint me once, I didn't know any better. . . ." The voice seemed to dissolve into tears for a few moments. Then, after a brief pause, it returned. "How soon can you get the key?"

"I . . . I don't know where she keeps it. . . ."

"Then you must look!" demanded the voice impatiently. "The old woman means to harm you, Pandora. She means to put you here, in my place. My time is almost over; I get weaker every day. . . ."

"But why should she wish to hurt me?" cried Pandora. "What have I done to her?"

"Nothing . . . but you see, by putting you in here, she goes on living, looking young and healthy."

"Oh, lord! Surely . . . surely that's not the secret she's forever talking about. No, I can't believe it!"

"You *will* believe it! You *must!*"

"But . . . no, no! I'm getting out of this crazy house before it kills me. . . . I'll send help for you, Ellen, but I'm afraid to stay here any longer."

"Wait! You don't understand. . . . You can't send help to me. Don't you see, now that they've got you here, they'll never let you escape. They must be watching you all the time. . . . Maybe they're even doing it now."

"But why should they? As far as they know, I'm in the dark about it all. . . ."

"Even if you could get away, she'll fetch you back. She'll send *him* to get you. You won't escape that kind of evil by running away!"

"Then what can I do?"

"Trust me. Find that key. I'll do the rest. I'm the one person that the old woman is afraid of."

"Afraid? Why. . . ?"

"That's why she keeps me caged up here, because she's afraid that one day I'll get out and find her. I've nearly done it a couple of times! That thing on the door is supposed to keep me bottled up, but when I concentrate, really concentrate, I can get to her. . . . I can make the cat fall down and then I can worm my mind through every crack in the door until I find her . . . but it takes so long and there's always somebody on hand to help her. Believe me, Pandora, the only way to do this thing is for you to help me! What do you say?"

Pandora stood there uncertainly, shaking her head from side to side.

"Look," she said at last. "Ellen . . . I've got to have time to think about this."

"There *is* no time," wailed the impatient voice on the other side of the door. "Take my word for it. If we don't do something in the next couple of days, then we may as well not bother!"

"But it's so hard to understand . . . all of this. You can't expect me to just go along with it. I mean, I don't even know who you are. You could be anybody. . . ."

"I told you! My name is Ellen Hughes. I used to live in the village of Brechfa, until the old woman took me. I lived in a little cottage with my Mother and Father. . . ."

"Are you trying to tell me that they haven't looked for you?" demanded Pandora incredulously.

"Of course they must have looked! But how would they know I was here? I was just taken, while I was walking in the forest one day. That horrible, dark-haired man, Ewen, I think she calls him . . . he tricked me; told me some story about an imp in a bottle, that he had up at the house. Asked me if I'd like to see it. . . . I never thought . . . I said yes. And there I met the lady and she seemed nice and friendly. And she said, would I like to have my picture painted and I said, 'yes, please!' And the man sat down and did it there and then; it only took an hour or so. . . . It was beautiful, so beautiful. They made me wear a nightgown and sit on a bed in a little room, with all my hair untied, and when I saw the picture, it was like a mirror, it seemed so real. . . ."

Pandora saw with vivid detail the portrait that had so taken her fancy on her first evening in the house; and felt horribly cold and small and she thought that she was beginning to understand at last, though the vague answer that was forming itself in the cobwebs of her mind seemed more fantastic than all the madness that Bryn Myrrdin had given her already.

Her voice was barely a whisper as she asked,

"Ellen . . . when did all this happen?"

But Ellen must not have heard through the thick oak door, because she continued in her sad, little voice.

"I couldn't understand it. . . . They'd been so nice and friendly; but when I said that I ought to be going home they wouldn't let me. They took me up to this room . . . this horrible bare room . . . and they shut me in, without even a light, though I howled and screamed and banged on the door. All the while I could hear them outside, moving about, mumbling. Then . . . oh, then. . . ."

Once again her voice subsided into a flood of bitter tears.

Pandora waited, her body and mind numb. She seemed to see before her eyes, a great, scrawled signature and a date; Nineteen-eighteen. She was somehow afraid to repeat her last question, because she was sure that the answer would be that same, inexplicable date. She had to ask, just the same.

"Ellen?"

A sniff. A pause. "Yes?"

"Can . . . can you remember when it was they took you?"

"A long time ago. I can't tell. It's so hard to remember back. . . ."

"Well, roughly. You said *years*." She took a deep breath. "How many?"

A long, tired sigh. "Very, very long time. . . ." Another pause. "So hard to remember . . . the war was nearly over, I know that. We were expecting to see my brother again before too long. He'd been away, fighting in France . . . almost four years he'd been gone. I remember Mother mentioning a place called . . . Mons . . . something like that. . . ."

Pandora felt like she'd been punched in the chest. She must have fallen silent, because Ellen's voice called out.

"Pandora! Are you still there?"

"Yes . . . yes, I'm still here." She struggled to control her reeling mind. "All that happened sixty years ago, Ellen," she said tonelessly.

The reply seemed only mildly surprised.

"Oh. As long as that, then. I thought it seemed like a long time. . . ."

Pandora tried vainly to match up the lost, little girl's voice with the face and body of a sixty-year-old woman. It didn't work. Not for a moment. Somehow, Ellen's age had been suspended. The passing of the years seemed not to have affected her.

"You *will* help me, won't you?" whispered Ellen, from her dark prison.

"Yes. Yes, of course. . . . I don't quite know how, but I'll help. The first thing is to get hold of that key, if you think it's the only way. If I can just. . . ."

She broke off abruptly and whirled around at the sound of a footstep behind her, she found herself looking at Ewen. He was looking at her intently and there was not a trace of compassion on his face. In the harsh glare of the hall light, his face seemed more evil than ever. He began to approach her, his arms outstretched.

The suddenness of his appearance galvanised her into instinctive action. She snatched Geraint's torch from her back pocket and without a second thought for his motives, she flung it full into his face. He hardly seemed to notice it, though it glanced off his temple with a loud crack. He just kept right on coming. At the last second, Pandora ducked beneath his grasp and slipped through his legs. Then she ran hell-bent for leather towards the stairway, in the hot flood of fear that had suddenly taken her. With a yell, Ewen reeled about and came lumbering along the landing in pursuit.

Pandora reached the wooden screen and fumbled helplessly for a moment with the swinging board, all too aware of Ewen's footsteps thudding down a few scant feet behind her. Suddenly, the board opened up and she flung herself through the gap. Her forehead dashed against something with stunning force and her head seemed to explode with fireworks. She hesitated, stood reeling at the top of the stairs, as her surroundings seemed to lurch and weave before her. From the corner of her eye she was dimly aware of Ewen's powerful figure emerging from the darkness.

"Escape!" The one word filled the aching vacuum of her consciousness. She took a hesitant step forward, then another, broke into a stumbling, shuffling run.

Then there was nothing under her feet anymore and she was falling in horrible, stomach-churning slow motion and, a long way off, a familiar voice was screaming.

A fuzzy, indistinct hardness came whirling up to meet her and she was about to fling up her hands to ward it off, when the world exploded with a sudden, spasmodic jolt and she realised that the hardness was now soft and that she was sinking into it, leaving no ripples in the blackness.

Chapter Fourteen

Red.

Everything was red. She seemed to float in a crimson tide and she was neither awake nor asleep. A thick, choking nausea hung heavy on her stomach. From far away, hollow metallic voices came drifting in on the viscous air. Curious, she paused in her unconsciousness to listen to them.

"I think she's all right. . . ." Ewen's voice, strained and anxious.

"You idiot! You could have killed her! What d'you think you were doing?" Aunt Rachel, very, very angry.

"I heard someone moving about up there. Ever the watchdog, you see. . . ."

"What was she doing, for God's sake?"

"She seemed to be talking."

"Talking? You mean. . . ?"

"I think so. That's what it seemed like."

"Impossible . . . it's not possible. . . . Well, don't *stand* there, fool; get her to bed and then go for the doctor. By hell fire, if you've harmed her, I'll make you wish you'd never been born! Careful!"

Hands. Gentle hands, holding her secure, lifting her up, carrying her along for what seemed an eternity. Then placing her down onto soft warmth and arranging more warmth over her.

Stroking her fevered head. Willing her to sleep. She fought against it for a few moments, but she was very tired, so very, very tired, and gradually, the redness eased itself down to a deep, rich earth colour, then a soft, empty grey and finally, to blackness once again.

She opened her eyes.

It seemed that she was outside now, because above her, a great, pale moon peered down from a curtain of darkness. She blinked furiously, focussed her gaze; the moon became a pale, oval face, the kindly good-natured face of a plump, slightly-balding, middle-aged gentleman.

"Well, hello there!" said the face in a rich Welsh accent, and it winked one twinkling eye at her.

Pandora tried to speak. "Uh . . . what er. . . ."

"Easy now! A bit of a knock you've had, young lady, and it's best you stay calm."

Now Pandora realised that the face was attached to a neck and this, in turn, was attached to a stout, tweed-suited body. She also became aware of the peering figure of Aunt Rachel, hovering vulture-like, in the background.

She tried to speak again, though it was hard to control her voice.

"Uh . . . who. . . ?"

"Am I?" finished the stout gentleman with a smile. "Doctor Evans is my name. And you are Pandora, right?"

"Right. . . . What, uh. . . ? I can't. . . remember. . . ."

"I'm afraid it is down the stairs you have fallen, love. A nasty bang on the bonce you gave yourself and a lovely collection of bruises, but no bones broken, thank goodness! You'll have to take things easy for a couple of days, I think."

"Stairs. . . ." Abruptly, it all came flooding back to her; her conversation with Ellen, the appearance of Ewen, and then the fall. It was a wonder she wasn't dead! She tried to sit up, but that caused a paroxysm of dizziness and she was obliged to flop down on her pillow again.

"Hey, steady on, now!" advised Doctor Evans. "You're not going anywhere, just yet."

Pandora sighed. She studied the doctor earnestly for a few moments, noting the quiet friendliness in his eyes.

"He might listen," she thought to herself. "If I can just talk to him for a few minutes." First, though, she'd have to get rid of Aunt Rachel. She tried to organise her muddled thoughts without much success.

"How on earth did you come to fall downstairs?" asked Doctor Evans.

"I, uh . . . could I have a drink of water, please?" Pandora was aware of Aunt Rachel's staring eyes and found herself unable to talk with the old woman present.

"Here." The doctor handed her a glass from beside the bed and she sipped at it, then returned it to him. She had hoped to make it necessary for Aunt Rachel to go out to the bathroom, thus giving her a chance to confide in her new ally.

"How long will I have to stay in bed?" she asked.

"At least a day or two, I am afraid. Your Great Aunt will be giving you a sedative from time to time . . . something to make you sleep."

"Sleep . . . oh, no! I mustn't. . . ." Once again, Pandora tried to struggle upright but Doctor Evans held her shoulders and eased her gently down onto the pillow.

"Look," he chided her, "not to get all excited now! Rest is the best cure for you, girl, take my word. What's so important that you can't take it easy for a little while?"

"Yes," murmured Aunt Rachel. "I'd like to know the answer to that myself." She walked over to the bed and gazed at Pandora calmly.

"It's just . . . oh, I don't know. . . ." Pandora felt the silent accusation in Aunt Rachel's eyes and her voice trailed away miserably.

Doctor Evans chuckled, patted her on the head.

"I understand," he said. "When you are young, it does seem a terrible thing to be stuck in bed for a few days; but let's have no more fuss. Very lucky you are, that it won't be a few *months*." He began to place various bottles in his black leather case.

"You're not going, are you?" cried Pandora.

"Indeed I am, young lady! Back to my own bed, where I was sleeping soundly not one hour ago. You'll be all right. . . ."

"But you can't go yet!"

The doctor paused in his actions and looked at Pandora in surprise.

"Why not?" he inquired.

"Because I . . . I . . . ." Pandora glanced at Aunt Rachel and noticed that she wore an expression of undisguised fury.

"Because?" prompted Doctor Evans.

Pandora steeled herself to continue. "It's just that I have to talk to you . . . alone, if you don't mind."

Doctor Evans looked very uncomfortable. "Well, er . . . I hardly see. . . ." He gave Aunt Rachel an apologetic look.

"That's quite all right, Doctor." Her voice was surprisingly calm and her previous look of anger was masked by a sickly smile. "I must confess that I was half expecting something of this nature. You see, it's just as I told you earlier . . . perhaps it would do her good to chat to you about it. I'll be downstairs when you're through." With that, she wheeled around and made for the door; but just before she went out, she glanced back at Pandora with a curious smile, that looked somehow to be an expression of mocking triumph.

Pandora stared after her as the door slammed.

"What . . . what did she mean by that?"

Doctor Evans smiled reassuringly. "Oh . . . it is just that she has told me about your problem."

"My what?"

"Well, what should we call it? The times when your imagination plays tricks, gets the better of you. Does that seem a better description?"

Pandora shook her foggy head.

"I'm sorry, I don't quite. . . ."

Abruptly, it dawned on her what had happened. Anticipating that Pandora might seize the opportunity to confide in someone, Aunt Rachel had prepared the way by inventing tales of insanity and delusion. It was painfully apparent that anything Pandora might say now would be interpreted as one of the symptoms of her strange malady.

"Why that horrible old witch!" exclaimed Pandora bitterly. "It's not fair that she should make up such horrible lies about me! Now you won't even listen. . . ."

"But of course I'll listen."

"No! No, you won't, not really. You'll listen as a doctor and you won't hear *anything!* Don't you see, if you think I'm mad, you'll just say to yourself, 'Ah, she's raving!' "

Doctor Evans stroked his chin thoughtfully.

"Just steady on a minute now," he said. "Nobody is saying you are mad at all. Why don't you just tell me what is troubling you?"

Pandora lay back on her pillow for a few moments, looking searchingly into the doctor's face.

"I don't know where to begin," she sighed. "There's so much to tell and it's all fantastic; I don't think you'll believe a word of it."

Doctor Evans shrugged. "Try me," he suggested.

"Well . . . all right. Firstly . . . firstly, Aunt Rachel isn't what she seems. She is a terrible, evil woman and she plans to harm me."

"Stop right there! Let us just consider that statement for a moment. If your Great Aunt really wants to harm you, why did she call for me when you were injured? Hmm? Why didn't she just leave you where you lay?"

"Ah, but you see, you don't understand. She needs me alive and well. She has to lock me away in the upstairs room. You're shaking your head, but I know better! There's a room upstairs and, right at this moment, the old woman is keeping a little girl prisoner in it."

"Here, steady on a bit!"

"It's true, honestly. You can go up there and check on it, if you like. I've talked to her; her name is Ellen Hughes."

The doctor's eyes widened and then narrowed.

"Go on," he suggested.

"Did . . . did you notice how young my Great Aunt looks? She's at least eighty and you wouldn't think to look at her that she's a day over forty-five. . . . Am I right?"

"Absolutely. Quite remarkable it is, too; but surely not a crime?"

"It's done by magic."

"Magic, you say?"

"Yes. You see, Ewen . . . that's the gardener . . . is really . . . well, you've heard of Myrrdin, I suppose?"

"I should hope so."

"That's who he is. Don't ask me to explain that, because I hardly understand it myself. I just happen to know the truth . . . see, he's got this way of . . . kind of extracting the youth from little girls and he gives it to Aunt Rachel, to help her look like she does. He locks them in a room upstairs where Ellen is now and he's planning to do the same to me any day. I only know this because Ellen told me about it. . . . You see, first there has to be a picture of me and . . . oh, what's the use? You don't believe a word of this!"

Doctor Evans frowned and stroked his thinning hair.

"That would depend on what you mean by 'believe,'" he replied calmly. "Quite sure I am, that *you* believe it all; so, by that token, it must be real enough, I suppose."

Pandora shook her head desperately.

"That's just a nice way of saying I'm crazy," she muttered. "I don't blame you, either. . . . Sometimes, I wonder myself. Is it possible, doctor? Could I really be insane and imagining everything? What with those voices in my head all the time. . . ."

"Voices?" echoed Doctor Evans. "Tell me about them."

"Well . . . they seem to belong to children . . . the ones that have been killed before me, I think. They're always telling me to do things, lately."

"What kind of things. Wicked? Hurtful?"

"Oh, no! Nothing like that. In fact, when I wanted to get away from here, they said that I should stay. They kept nagging on at me all night, so that I couldn't sleep."

The doctor looked somewhat perplexed.

"Pandora . . . would you like to go home?" he suggested.

"Yes. More than anything else in the world. When I first started finding things out, it was fun, like being a detective. . . . Now, I'm frightened. I know that they don't want me to leave this house. Oh, but Doctor Evans, what can I do? The voices won't let me leave . . . and I promised Ellen that I'd try to help her escape. I told her that I'd get the police but she said no, it had to be me. Now I'm stuck here and she says that if she doesn't get out in the next couple of days, then she'll never escape." Pandora grabbed Doctor Evans's arm. "If only you'd go up there and talk to her!" she cried. "Then you'd have to believe me!"

"Easy now." The doctor squeezed her hand reassuringly. "I believe you, Pandora . . . at least, I don't think you are lying to me. You know, I think it would be best if you went home, just as soon as you are well." He stood up. "You get some sleep now," he suggested. "A few words I'm going to have, with your Great Aunt."

"Ask her . . . about the letter from my Mummy," suggested Pandora. "The one she kept from me . . . the one she opened and read. . . ."

A sudden tide of exhaustion seemed to flood through her aching limbs and her voice trailed away. She closed her eyes for a moment and then murmured again.

"Ask her . . . about the . . . letter. . . ."

Doctor Evans stood for several moments, looking down at the pale child on the bed. There was a troubled expression on his face. Something in the girl's confused raving was bothering him, a powerful quality of conviction that he found hard to shrug off.

It was obvious that the child was genuinely afraid of the two other members of the household. There was another strange thing; the name, Ellen Hughes. He knew the name, of course, and the local mystery that was connected with it, and it was possible that Pandora had heard mention of it during her brief visit to Bryn Myrrdin. It would have been easy to weave the story into the fabric of her insanity if, indeed, she really was disturbed. But then, wasn't there something horribly alien in the claustrophobic atmosphere of this old house, anyway, something that even he, a man of science if ever there was one, could feel, tickling like a spider's leg at the base of his spine. In all his years of work in the village of Brechfa, he had never once had occasion to call at this tumble-down old building. He had scoffed many times at the superstitious mumblings of many of his older acquaintances, when the subject of Savannah was touched upon. But now, standing alone beneath the cold and creaking beams of the ancient building, he could perhaps attach a little more credence to their stories. There was a profound sense of timelessness in the house, a brooding, foreboding atmosphere of mystery and guilt.

He sighed, touched his fingers to the girl's hot forehead. She was sleeping now, buried deep in a raging fever dream. Perhaps the sedatives would prove to be unnecessary. He picked up his bag and walked to the door.

It was ludicrous, but he was taken with an abrupt and powerful urge to have a look up in that disused top floor of the house. As an educated man, he could hardly allow himself to be led by what the child had told him; and yet . . . he remembered the way she'd referred to "Ellen." So sure. So afraid. . . .

For some reason, a violent shiver ran through his body, despite his warm clothes. "Ridiculous," he muttered. "There couldn't be anything up there."

"Ask her. . . ." murmured Pandora, deep in silent dreams.

Doctor Evans frowned. "What harm can it do?" he asked himself. "If I just slip up there . . . just to set my mind at rest, so to speak. . . ."

He reached out and opened the door.

Ewen stood before him. He was cleaning his fingernails with a long knife and he was smiling.

The corridor loomed ahead.

Pandora could see no end to it for it seemed to stretch away forever, grim and oppressive. She forced herself to run forward, though her limbs were leaden and a great tiredness snatched at her body. The steady, rhythmic clumping of her feet on the tiles seemed to explode like jungle drums in her head.

Escape! That was her purpose now; to flee this place of insanity into which she had delivered herself. The sweat hung thick on her fevered brow and her breaths came in shallow, shuddering gasps.

She seemed to run for a long, aching eternity; and always the corridor led onwards, in cold concrete silence. Then, quite abruptly, and without any warning, she was up in the open air and moving along the gravel path to the gates of Savannah.

There, on the grey road, a black saloon car was waiting. She paused hesitantly, for she had not expected to meet with anyone. But then, through the window, she recognised the smiling face of Doctor Evans. He flung open the door on the passenger side and, gratefully, Pandora slipped into the comfortable seat beside him. It was going to be all right now.

Doctor Evans gunned the engine and the car accelerated away, beneath the shadowy canopy of trees. Pandora smiled easily and relaxed. She was going home, back to the relative security of her Mother and the sharp, ironic humour of her Father. She was leaving behind the cold embrace of evil that had so nearly claimed her forever.

She smiled gratefully at Doctor Evans, but he was intent on

the road ahead. He sat hunched over the steering wheel and his expression was one of worry. They had emerged from the trees now and the road they followed was winding and treacherous, with a sheer drop on the left side and a high, rocky wall on the right. Pandora thought this rather strange, for she had not noticed anything like it on the way over from Carmarthen station; surely that was where they were heading?

She glanced back at Doctor Evans to ask about this, but now his face was nicely pale and he was looking into his driving mirror.

Slowly, Pandora turned around.

In the back seat sat Ewen and Aunt Rachel. They were both smiling at Pandora, a hideous, mocking display of triumph that chilled her to the marrow. She turned away to shout a warning to Doctor Evans, only to see that he was transfixed and that his nerveless hands had dropped from the steering wheel and that the car had careened over to the left and was dipping forward, into the waiting air.

She could see quite plainly a vista of trees and fields, stretched like a child's model, hundreds of feet below.

Then she was falling for the second time that night.

She woke with a gasp.

She was hot and sticky with sweat and she felt so weak that she could hardly move a muscle. Her eyes were wet with tears and a thought kept turning over and over in her mind.

"Poor Doctor Evans . . . poor Doctor Evans. It's all my fault. . . ."

The dream had seemed so real.

She became aware of the soft padding of footsteps in the room and realised that whoever had entered must have awakened her. Supposing nobody had broken the dream, she wondered? Would she have continued with that terrible fall through the air, until her frail body was smashed like a doll, in the wreckage of the car? Would she never have awakened again?

Aunt Rachel's face floated into her line of vision. She stood observing Pandora closely, her features devoid of any emotion whatsoever.

"Where . . . where is . . . Doctor Evans?" gasped Pandora.

"Gone," said Aunt Rachel simply.

"He . . . was going to talk . . . to you."

"Really? How very interesting. Unfortunately, it seems he had a rather pressing appointment somewhere else." She reached down and stroked Pandora's forehead. "I declare, you are burning up, child!" she murmured. There was genuine concern in her voice. "Here, now." She slipped a small pill into Pandora's mouth and tilted a glass of water to her lips. Pandora tried to struggle but there was little she could do.

"There," crooned Aunt Rachel. "You must get some rest. In a couple of days you'll be as good as new." And she turned away and went out of the room.

Pandora lay still in silent frustration as her senses began to shut down one by one. The room seemed to melt, vibrate, shimmer, reform itself in a puzzle of colours. She cursed herself for not taking the chance to escape when it had presented itself. Instead, she had let herself be guided by some half-heard, unidentified voices. She had badly underestimated the danger into which she had unwittingly travelled. Now she was at Aunt Rachel's mercy, drugged and incapable of fighting back in any way. She wondered if Ewen even *wanted* to help her. Even if he did, he seemed incapable of crossing the old woman in any way, so long as she possessed the charm.

The room darkened perceptibly; she became aware of a thudding rhythm, soft and barely audible at first, but gradually growing in volume, until it seemed to crash and reverberate through her head. She realised, with a sense of surprise, that she was listening to the beating of her own heart. Her breath seemed to wheeze like a pile of autumn leaves in her chest. She wondered vaguely if she was going to die; but at that moment, the drugs finally took purchase of her mind and winged her away, into the dark, silent sanctuary of oblivion.

Chapter Fifteen

She might have slept for eternity or just a few short hours.

When she woke again, the room was bright with sunshine, though the window was tight shut against its warm invitation. She still felt groggy and weak but, with some considerable effort, she managed to sit herself up, fumble with the catch and, after some minutes' work, open the window, allowing a flood of fresh perfumed air into the staleness of the room. She fell back and breathed deeply.

She had never felt so utterly helpless in her life. Trapped here in this way, she had simply no hope of escape. She seriously doubted whether she had the strength to stand, let alone walk. Her one chance lay with Doctor Evans; after all, had he not said that Pandora should be allowed to return home? If only he would call again, drive her away from Savannah, just as he had in the dream. . . .

Ah, yes, the dream. What had that meant? The abrupt and horrible ending, the plunge into space . . . that too, had seemed so real. She considered, not for the first time, the possibility that *everything* was part of an impossibly complex nightmare. If only she might wake again in a few moments, to discover that she was home in bed and that she had never left the everyday sanity of London.

The bedroom door opened and Aunt Rachel entered. She

looked slightly surprised to see that Pandora was awake but, after a brief hesitation, she approached the bed, smiling like a Cheshire cat.

Pandora was overcome with revulsion at the old woman's hypocrisy.

"Keep away from me!" she cried. "Just go away!"

Aunt Rachel stopped, frowned.

"Now, now, Pandora. . . ." she began.

"Now, nothing! How *dare* you pretend with me? I know everything; I know what you're planning to do to me and I hate you!"

"What are you saying?"

"I know about Ellen Hughes. I've talked to her. . . ."

"No!" Aunt Rachel's face seemed to contort with fury and there was an indescribable look of fear in her eyes. "That's not possible! She couldn't speak to you . . . to anyone. She's not even *alive!*"

"Oh, but she is," replied Pandora calmly. "And you are afraid of her for some reason; I can see that. . . . But, Aunt Rachel, why? Why are you going to do these things to me? I've done nothing to hurt you."

Aunt Rachel shook her head. There was not a trace of emotion on her face.

"Don't be foolish, girl," she sneered. "D'you think it's a personal thing? Let me tell you, any girl of the right age would do just as well. Of course, I've always kept you in mind. I read a magazine article about your Father several years ago. It mentioned a nine-year-old daughter. Why else would I have chosen to write to him, do you suppose? To me you were nothing more than one of several irons in the fire. I'd all but given up hope of engineering our meeting, even had a local child under scrutiny. I had everything planned, down to the last exact detail. . . . Then fate stepped in and delivered you right into my lap. I'd have been a fool not to have taken such an opportunity."

"But I don't understand." Pandora's voice shook with emotion. "You've had your life . . . a good, long life. . . . Why do you want more? What reason have you got to go on?"

"Reason? What are you babbling about?"

"Surely there has to be a reason to live, Aunt Rachel? Otherwise, there's just no point. . . . Look at your life here, alone in this cold place. Never going out, afraid to even walk in the fresh, clean air. All the time you spend in that foul, dark room of yours, alone with your thoughts, or with Ewen, who must hate you to the bottom of his soul. What is there here for you? Myfanwy only stays because of the nice things you've bought her. I don't suppose you've got a single person to love you in the whole world. . . ."

Pandora broke off with an exclamation of pain as Aunt Rachel's hand smashed across her right cheek.

"Be still!" howled Aunt Rachel, in a voice that was torn ragged with anguish. "Do you imagine I *enjoy* it, child? You don't understand! To me, life is not a thing to relish, to enjoy. . . . It is a drug! A drug I crave, a drug I need, a drug I *will* have, no matter what the cost." She turned away for a moment and when she spoke again, her voice was small and fearful. "I dare not die. . . . Death is my constant fear; my soul is damned to the flames of hell forever. . . ."

"People can be forgiven."

"No. Not after the things I've done. . . ." She whirled around again. "Damn it, I don't want anyone's forgiveness!"

"You won't win," reasoned Pandora. "You'll be found out. When I don't go home, people will come looking for me. Do you think my parents will rest, until they find out what's happened to me?"

Aunt Rachel smiled tiredly. "And don't you think that Ellen's parents came looking for *her*?" she murmured. "But this is a big, wild country, Pandora; little children can wander abroad and come to grief. There's a thousand potholes to fall into, a hundred lakes to drown in. . . . Your parents will receive a phone call. There will be three distraught witnesses to claim that you went for a stroll in the woods and never returned. There will be a short search. And then, of course, your body will be found!"

"My . . . body . . . ?"

Aunt Rachel smiled sweetly. "You will have suffered an accident. A fall from a high place, perhaps . . . such a shame. Your parents will bear the body homewards, overcome with grief, taking all those troublesome photographers and reporters in their wake. Nobody will, for one moment, suspect that you are, in fact, still *here in this house!*"

"But how? How?"

"I didn't expect for one moment that you would understand, my dear. It has something to do with a coffin, hidden away upstairs. Ewen built it for you only a few days ago. . . . You see, in a way, it will be your coffin. You shall lie in it . . . and yet you won't. A very old process, its origins lost in time. It worked for Ellen, and it will work for you, Pandora. And you know what? You have Ewen to thank for it all! If it weren't for his skills, I would be dead and buried by now. Ah, but he's a special kind of man! Have you any idea how powerful he is? A couple of words from him would send any potential snoopers out into the night, raving. He can make a person see darkness in the middle of the day . . . turn a man's brain inside out and throw it to the four winds. And yet, when I say the word, he's as tame as any puppy licking at my feet!"

"He won't help you. He wants to help me!"

Aunt Rachel laughed derisively. "Sure he does," she admitted. "But poor little Ewen does what he's told." She took a glass phial from the sleeve of her dress and extracted a single white pill. "And now," she announced, "it's time for you to sleep, once again." She reached out and grasped Pandora firmly by the hair.

"No! I won't take it! I won't!" Pandora lashed out at Aunt Rachel with all the strength she could muster into her feeble arms, but the old woman was surprisingly powerful. Holding Pandora back against the pillow with one arm, she forced the pill between Pandora's clenched teeth with her free hand and then grasped her victim's nose tightly, until she was forced to take in air and swallow.

"There, now." Aunt Rachel straightened up and smoothed her rumpled hair into place. "You see, Pandora, it's quite useless to try and fight me. You won't win, no matter how hard you try."

Pandora lay on her pillow, sobbing with helpless fear and rage.

"We'll see," she ventured bravely.

The bedroom door opened and Ewen entered, carrying a small artist's easel and a large, framed canvas. He began to set up the easel at the foot of the bed, his face impassive.

"Well, we're finally going to get that portrait done," announced Aunt Rachel cheerfully. "So refreshingly different, don't you think? The subject pictured frail and innocent in the depths of sleep. . . . It will look so lovely in the sitting room. . . ."

The world seemed to be whizzing around a vortex in the centre of Pandora's head and Aunt Rachel's voice was like an echoing screech of triumph in her ears. She wanted so much to reply to those taunting words but all she could do for the moment was to fight grimly against the black, swirling clouds that came creeping in to claim her once again. . . .

She no longer knew anything for sure.

She seemed to be awake and it was nighttime now, because the window above her was an oblong of black velvet, decorated with tiny glittering rhinestones. Ewen's easel was gone; had he finished the portrait already, she wondered, or was this simply another vivid dream? There was a curiously numb sensation throughout the length of her body and she couldn't even feel the mattress against her back. It was as though she was suspended scant inches above the surface of the bed and there was a thin layer of warm air between her body and the sheets, so that she was touching nothing. It was a decidedly unnerving experience.

She was suddenly aware of a presence inside the room and, glancing up, she saw the ghost boy standing at the foot of her bed, his naked body white and spectral in the gloom. She had never seen him this closely before, and a brief thrill of horror clutched at her heart when she realised why his stare had always seemed so expressionless from a distance. He had no eyes. Instead, the lids opened onto twin pits of empty blackness. Despite this, Pandora felt no fear at his nearness. He was smiling reassuringly at her and it was quite obvious that he could somehow see perfectly well. He began to beckon to her with one hand, indicating that she should get out of bed. She shook her head, feeling that this was hardly possible in her present, weak condition, but the boy continued urging her to try.

To her great surprise, she found that she could indeed sit up, although it required considerable effort. She pushed the blankets aside and swung her legs out onto the floor. Sparks of pain danced through her shins and she grimaced. The boy nodded and moved away towards the door, beckoning her to follow. Slowly, painfully, she eased herself into a standing position and began to hobble after him; then she paused in amazement as he simply vanished into thin air. She hesitated for a moment, unsure of what to do, but a force still seemed to will her onwards. She limped over to the door and grasped the handle. She was surprised to find that it was unlocked. She eased the door open a fraction and peered out onto the landing, only to see Aunt Rachel emerging from her room and heading off along the landing, in the direction of the top-floor staircase. Almost the instant that the old woman had disappeared from view, the ghost boy materialised by Aunt Rachel's door. Once again, he beckoned to Pandora, a look of intense urgency on his face.

Taking a deep breath, Pandora forced herself to walk towards him, though her limbs were as heavy as lead. After what seemed an eternity she reached the door of her Great Aunt's room. It was slightly ajar and a low light burned within. Cautiously, Pandora creaked it open and looked inside.

Thankfully, it was quite empty and she went on inside, gazing around at the horrible mildewed walls and the cobweb-festooned ornaments that littered the place. It looked as though it hadn't seen a cleaner's brush in over fifty years. Cockroaches skittered here and there across the rotting carpets and, occasionally, a small grey mouse emerged from behind an item of furniture. Pandora wondered how Aunt Rachel could stand to spend even a few minutes inside such a revolting place, let alone hour after hour.

The ghost boy drifted in beside her. She could feel a distinct chill emanating from him; yet she knew that in some way he was trying to help her. They approached a large dressing table. Pandora was fascinated to see only her own reflection in the dusty mirror. The ghost boy indicated the top of the dressing table, which was littered with grubby bottles and dust-laden trinkets. In the centre of these was a large wooden casket, set on a circular board, which was decorated with strange diagrams and Latin words. The ghost boy pointed to this several times and mimed the action of lifting its lid.

"You . . . want me to do it?" whispered Pandora, and the boy nodded.

Shaking her head to dispell the traces of dizziness that lingered there, she reached out and lifted the lid of the casket. It opened easily. Inside, nestled on a cushion of black velvet, there lay a large brass key.

Suddenly, she had the distinct impression that this was the key to Ellen's room, the one she had been told to procure. She snatched it up and closed the lid, wondering if the possession of it would do her any good at this stage. She turned to address a question to the ghost boy, but he had vanished. Quickly, she turned and made her way out of the room, leaving the door as she had found it. She began to plod wearily back in the direction of her room, every nerve in her body screaming out for rest. About halfway there, she became aware of footsteps clumping down the rickety old staircase at the end of the corridor. She panicked, tried to break into a run, missed her footing and sprawled onto the floor. Her heart missed several beats. Glancing up, the door to her room seemed a hundred miles away. The approaching footsteps seemed to echo in her head. With a titanic effort, she lunged to her feet and ran in a weaving, drunken line along the landing. She could almost picture Aunt Rachel on the bottommost step, about to turn the corner. With seconds to spare, she dived in through the doorway, closing the door after her. Then she dived into bed, pulled the covers over herself and slid the key beneath her pillow. She feigned sleep.

Moments later, the door to her room opened. Aunt Rachel's voice cursed softly, then yelled, "Ewen! Dammit, didn't I tell you to keep this door locked?"

There was a sharp click as a key turned.

Receding footsteps.

Silence.

Pandora remembered to breathe again. Beneath the pillow, her fingers caressed cold metal. It was the most precious thing in her possession at this moment and for the first time in ages, she drifted off to sleep in a hopeful frame of mind.

Chapter Sixteen

It was Myfanwy's voice that woke her.

Pandora lay blinking uncertainly in the pale, morning sunlight as the stout housekeeper bustled into the room, carrying a breakfast tray before her. She was humming a melody to herself, just as she always did and her happy carefree nature seemed to belie any of the incidents that had occurred in the last couple of days.

"Good morning, good morning!" she called. "And what mischief have you been up to while I was gone?"

"Hello, Myfanwy. . . ." Pandora managed to prop herself up against her pillows and receive the tray of toast and bacon and eggs; the aroma of it reminded her that she was ravenously hungry, for Aunt Rachel had not bothered to make any provision for her young appetite. She set to eating without further ado. Myfanwy sat herself down at the foot of the bed.

"Feeling better this morning?" she inquired.

Pandora nodded, for her mouth was too full to reply. She studied Myfanwy's kind face for a moment and wondered just how deeply this pleasant woman could be involved in Aunt Rachel's schemes. It seemed highly unlikely that she might be unaware of them.

"Aren't you the silly one, then?" chided Myfanwy. "Falling downstairs like that. However did you manage it?"

Pandora frowned and pushed her half-empty plate aside.

"What did Aunt Rachel say about it?" she asked.

"Well, only that playing about on the stairs, you were . . . and that you tripped over and fell. . . ."

"I see. She didn't say anything else?"

"What else was there to say?"

"That I'm being kept a prisoner in here . . . but then, you must realise that. You just had to unlock the door to get in, didn't you?"

Myfanwy averted her eyes for a few moments. "That . . . that's a silly notion," she muttered. Her face bore the guilty expression of an accomplice.

"Yes, you know about it all right," sighed Pandora. "Oh, Myfanwy . . . I thought, perhaps you . . . oh, I don't know. I suppose you'd have to be part of it, living here all the time."

"Why don't you finish your breakfast?" suggested Myfanwy.

"I don't feel hungry any more."

Myfanwy shook her head sadly. "Please not to judge me so harshly, miss," she retorted. "I'm not a wicked person, you see, not like . . . not like them. Only, they say things sometimes to frighten me . . . and I wouldn't dare go against them."

Pandora gripped Myfanwy's hands tightly.

"Yes, but . . . do you know what they're planning to do to me? Do you know half of what's happening here . . . about Ellen Hughes?"

Myfanwy looked away again, out of the small window.

"Oh, yes," she murmured. "Poor little mite. Of course, happened a long time before I came here, it did. Part of history, really. I suppose you don't know about Ellen's pool?"

"No, I don't."

"There's a place in the forest . . . a big lake, there is, very deep and muddy at the bottom. When Ellen Hughes disappeared all those years ago, a big search, they had, and after some days, the little girl's body was found floating in the pool. Her parents had a big stone put by the water's edge, telling the story of how she had wandered away from home and come to grief. Read it myself, I did, many times when I was a young girl. . . ."

"And you believed the story?"

"Yes, of course. I had no reason to think anything else . . . then. But I came to work at the house when I was in my late twenties. I suppose a few months it was, before I heard her crying in the night. Whenever I tried to mention it to Miss Ellis, a terrible rage she would fly into. 'Imagining things, you are,' she would tell me. But I heard, just the same . . . in the end, made my way up to that room, I did. That was when I found out who she was. . . ."

"And you did nothing?"

Myfanwy shook her head. "What could I do?" she replied. "It was already twenty years too late . . . and besides, there is something you don't know. See, before I was brought here from Brechfa, I had nothing at all. Very poor, my family was; me, my brothers and sisters and my poor Ma, God rest her soul. My Father died when I was three and left my Mother to bring up seven children. Sometimes we were lucky to have one meal a day. Well, when Miss Ellis took me on here, everything changed for me. Wages I was given, more money than I'd ever dreamed of owning. A fine kitchen to work in and all the food I could eat. People in the village, well-to-do people, started to take notice of me. . . . You know, Pandora, I can remember a time when I was very young . . . even younger than you. . . . I was standing alone in my Ma's dirty old house, with no shoes on my feet and no food in my belly and saying to myself, 'Lord, if ever out of this place I get, there will be no going back! Not ever!' And I meant what I said, even if I had to turn a blind eye now and then."

"Myfanwy! Do you realise what you're saying? Ellen Hughes was *murdered* in this house. Next, they'll murder me. Don't you even care?"

"Of course, I do . . . only . . . I'm not strong enough to do anything, girl. I suppose that you think I'm wicked, but I'm not, not really. Weak, I am, weak and frightened. And besides, there is something else . . . something that happened to me in the past. In many ways it makes me as bad as them. You see, when I was younger, not long after I came to work here, in fact . . . got involved, I did, with a man from the village. He . . . well, got me into trouble, you know? It was a terrible thing for me. I couldn't keep the baby; for various reasons it wasn't possible. Then . . . then Miss Ellis said she would help me out; give me . . . you know what an abortion is, I suppose?"

"Yes, of course."

Myfanwy's face mirrored the pain caused by her memory.

"Horrible, it was . . . the pain . . . unbelievable . . . and then, when I thought it was all over, Miss Ellis came to me and said that she knew who the Father was and that I'd better make sure I toed the line in future, or tell everyone, she would, and have me sent home in disgrace."

"You mean she blackmailed you? But Myfanwy, surely it couldn't have mattered enough to forget about what's been going on here?"

Myfanwy stared down at the floor.

"The baby's Father . . . was a priest," she said quietly. "When I told him that I was pregnant, he . . . he killed himself." Her voice was weak and tremulous. "I knew right from the start how wrong it was. But I went on with it just the same, because I loved . . . I couldn't let people know of such a thing! I couldn't! You know Ewen, you've seen what he is like. If she only said the word, he would kill me and think nothing of it. I've seen him do some terrible things over the years and I dare not go against him."

Pandora sighed. She lay back against her pillows.

"Well, that's it, then," she said blankly. "Myfanwy, what day is it?"

"Monday."

A cold chill ran down Pandora's spine. "It must be tonight," she murmured. "It was Friday when I overheard Aunt Rachel talking to Ewen . . . and then she said, 'three days.' I suppose the painting is finished?"

Myfanwy nodded glumly. "It's down in the sitting room," she said.

Pandora thought about Ellen. If any help was to be extended to her, it would have to be given that very evening or it would be too late; indeed, it might be too late already. She slid her hand surreptitiously beneath the pillow. Sure enough, the key was still there, cold and reassuring to her touch. That was the one small point in her favour at the moment. But how was she to get upstairs?

She glanced up and saw that Myfanwy was holding the same phial of pills that Aunt Rachel had been dosing her with.

"Oh, please Myfanwy," she cried, "don't make me take one of those things. I couldn't stand it!"

"Miss Ellis said. . . ."

"Look, what difference can it make? I'm locked in here, aren't I? It's not as if I can escape."

Myfanwy looked somewhat doubtful. "Well . . . no, I suppose not."

"Horrid things. It seems as though I've been asleep off and on, since Doctor Evans was here."

Myfanwy's expression changed in an instant, into one of extreme shock.

"Doctor Evans," she echoed. "He was here?"

"Yes."

"When?"

"Uh . . . Saturday, I think. I seem to be losing track of the time. What's the matter? Has something happened to him?"

She nodded. "Poor man. His car went off the road over beyond the hill. Right down a deep gulley it fell, and smashed to bits on the rocks below. Burnt to a crisp, he was, though no one can understand why he was out so late at night."

"Oh, no," whispered Pandora. She buried her face in her hands. "I know what he was doing there," she said tonelessly. "He'd been here, Myfanwy, to see me. Where do you think Aunt Rachel got those drugs from? I . . . talked to him, tried to tell him what was happening here . . . oh, don't you see? *They* killed him. Somehow, they made him drive off the road, made it look like an accident, just as they did with Ellen . . . just as they will with me! It's all my fault, Myfanwy, for trying to talk to him . . . that poor man. I dreamed about him. I dreamed I was in the car with him and it was probably happening as I saw it. . . ."

Myfanwy bowed her head.

"Now, do you understand?" she whispered hoarsely. "It's not that I don't *want* to help you. But if they found out . . . they'd kill me too, Pandora, I know they would." She took the breakfast tray and got up to go but Pandora grabbed her arm, insistently.

"Myfanwy! Please . . . you just can't leave me to fight them alone."

"I must!"

"If . . . if you'd just leave the door unlocked!"

"No, miss . . . I'm sorry, but please don't even ask!"

Gently, she prised Pandora's arm away and hurried out of the room, closing the door behind her. There was a few moments' silence and then, the soft scraping of a key, turning in the lock.

Pandora bit her lip, trying to arrange her feverish thoughts. She was not beaten yet, not by a long chalk. For a start, she had managed to evade those drugs, and while she was awake there was always a chance of escape. An idea came to her in a sudden flash of inspiration. It was so simple, it was a wonder that it hadn't occurred to her before. She would climb out of the window, down the ivy, just as she had done once before. Once out of Savannah, she would make her way down to Dreulfa and find help. She scrambled up onto her knees and undid the latch of the window, threw it open and glanced out. An exclamation of surprise escaped from her lips.

The wall below her had been methodically stripped bare of every single strand of foliage. All that remained was smooth, grey stone and a terrifying drop to the earth below.

Time passed.

Pandora sat on the bed with her head cradled in her hands. It was beginning to look as though she was beaten. After her discovery of the missing ivy, she had dressed herself and explored other avenues of escape. Firstly, she had spent several fruitless hours trying to pick the lock of her bedroom door with a variety of improvised tools and, as a final measure, she had even tried the brass key, but it proved to be far too large. Then she had remembered seeing a film in which a prisoner in similar circumstances had effected an escape from a high window by constructing a rope made of strips of blanket. Unfortunately, her own blankets proved to be far too tough to tear and when she had searched for her hair scissors and penknife, she found that they had been removed from the drawer of the dressing table where they had been left. She managed to make a rope of sorts, by tearing up the thin cotton sheets, but the result was such a flimsy affair that it would never have taken her weight and she would have been as well advised to simply jump from the window ledge. She had indeed considered that possibility several times, but the chances of escaping without breaking several bones were slim, to say the least, and such an outcome would be of no help to her whatsoever. Now she had come to the conclusion that there was nothing to do but wait for the end, the end that must inevitably come later that evening. She wondered dismally what time it was. Her watch had stopped days ago, but she judged it to be about five in the afternoon.

A sudden anger seemed to blossom up within her. Why should she wait so passively for the end, anyway? As long as she was alive, she had every chance of making it out, somehow. After all, hadn't she taken all the knocks so far? And if neither Ewen nor Myfanwy would aid her, then she would simply have to help herself.

And she still had the key.

She examined it thoughtfully, turning it around in her fingers. For the first time it struck her how fantastic had been the means by which she obtained it. She didn't doubt for one moment that it was, indeed, the key to Ellen's room; but she wondered if the possession of it could afford her any help at all. Supposing she did seize an opportunity to get up to the top floor and release Ellen from her place of confinement? What good could such an action achieve? Ellen sounded no more than a small, frail girl behind that heavy oak door and, once free, it was hard to imagine her being of any use against Aunt Rachel and Ewen. And yet, she had sounded so sure, so positive.

"Trust me," she had said. "Find that key. I'll do the rest. *I'm the one person that the old woman is afraid of.*"

Somehow, Pandora knew that this was so. She remembered the fearful tone in Aunt Rachel's voice when Ellen's name had been mentioned, only the previous day, and how she had been unwilling to accept the fact that Ellen was able to speak to Pandora. The problem was that time was fast running out. Precious time had been lost due to the accident and Ellen had stressed during their one conversation that a few days were all that was left to her.

Pandora sighed and stood up. She paced about the small room restlessly for a few minutes and then paused to gaze out of the window. The lawn looked bare and desolate and the afternoon sun was being gradually suffocated by great, tumbled pillars of bruise-black cloud, drifting in from the hills. The house itself seemed as grim and silent as the grave.

Pandora sat herself down on the bed again, feeling the increasing tenseness of fear and apprehension growing within her, coiling itself up like a huge clock spring in her stomach.

"Ewen," she murmured, "why won't you help me?"

The thought of his name revived memories of her recent sexual experience. A powerful guilt ignited within her. She had been about to condemn him as an evil man, but, in fact, she had enjoyed his advances, and so she must be evil, too. . . .

Her thoughts trailed away miserably, and she subsided into tears, her body shaking with grief. It was hopeless. It seemed as though every person who ever walked through the doorway of Savannah became tainted with wickedness and corruption.

After a few minutes her tears ceased to flow. She wiped at her eyes and walked aimlessly around the room again. She paused by the door and put her ear against it, but she could not discern a single sound anywhere in the big, silent house.

"Got to organise myself," she thought. She glanced around the bedroom for a suitable weapon to use as a last resort. Nothing seemed suitable until, after much deliberation, she upturned a wooden chair and pulled and twisted one of its legs until the seat splintered and she was left holding a hefty club with an evil chunk of jagged wood at one end. She examined it grimly, wondering if she would have the courage to use it when the time came. Violence had never been in her nature, but she could hardly allow herself to be taken without some kind of resistance.

She walked over to the window and looked out.

The sky had grown dark and venomous, so that it seemed to be much later in the day than it really was. A blustering wind was rattling the trees and shrubs in the garden, and occasional flurries of rain spattered the window with moisture. Pandora shivered. The weather seemed eminently suitable for the kind of drama that was to be enacted that evening.

Suddenly, she became aware of heavy footsteps coming up the staircase beyond her door. Her heart jumped violently in her chest and she stood her ground, rooted to the spot with fear. The footsteps approached, slow and irregular, then came to a halt in front of Pandora's room. There was a brief silence and then, a loud, scraping click as the key turned a slow revolution in the lock. Somehow, Pandora forced her legs to obey her, to carry her quickly and silently into the corner of the room, so that the door, when it opened, would conceal her. She held the improvised club before her with shaking, white-knuckled hands. The thudding of her heart seemed to fill the room with its rhythm of fear, and her mouth was as arid as a desert.

She swallowed hard and waited, hardly daring to breathe.

The door handle turned slowly around and then the door itself creaked open, cutting off Pandora's view. Now footsteps padded into the room and halted. The fingertips of a hand closed around the edge of the door, a woman's fingertips, with glossy, unpainted nails. Carefully, Pandora lifted the chair leg high above her head, knowing that she would have only one chance to strike. When that chance came, she must hit out with every ounce of strength she possessed and then run, run for her life. She drew one deep breath. The club felt like a bar of lead in her hands and she was dimly aware of several beads of sweat trickling down her forehead. She seemed to stand poised for the attack, a long, silent eternity, that could have been in reality, only a few, brief seconds.

Then, abruptly, a woman's head peered around the door.

Instinctively, Pandora jumped forward, then stopped dead in her tracks from sheer surprise. The descending chair leg snapped to a rigid halt, two inches above the head of an equally surprised Myfanwy. She was rather red-faced and seemed to be holding onto the door for support. Her voice was heavy and slurred as she said:

"Take it easy, Pandora, girl . . . come to get you out, I have."

Chapter Seventeen

Pandora was astonished. Myfanwy's attitude of only a few hours earlier had left the impression that no hope of any support could be expected from her. Now, here she stood, in the doorway, obviously much the worse for drink and with a different point of view altogether.

Pandora stepped forward and grasped Myfanwy's arm as the woman reeled unsteadily towards her. The powerful odour of gin was on her breath and she seemed to be in a mood of nervous agitation.

"Myfanwy!" exclaimed Pandora, mystified. "Are you all right?"

"Never felt better in my life," replied Myfanwy. "Dead drunk, I am, and a terrible shame, too, that I had to get myself into such a state before I could find the courage to help you. . . . Ah, God! Such a coward I've been. . . . After I was with you this morning I fell to thinking. Took a long look in the mirror and said to myself, 'Myfanwy, girl, if you sit back and let this thing happen, there'll be no peace for you in this world, nor any other, come to that.' Too long now, I've been turning a blind eye on the things that happen in this house. I've been too frightened to lose what I've got here. . . ." She chuckled and shook her head sadly. "Only trouble is," she murmured, "that I haven't really got anything. Not a thing. . . ." She spread her podgy hands and examined them carefully. "Why has it taken me so long to find that out?" she asked.

"It doesn't matter," replied Pandora. "You're here now, that's the main thing. Where . . . where are Aunt Rachel and Ewen?"

"They are out in the garage at the moment. Something wrong with the car, I think. . . . You know, you were right, Pandora, it was to happen tonight. Heard them talking, I did, out in the hallway. . . ." She pulled Pandora close to her. "You've got to get away from here," she whispered fiercely. "Just get as far away as you can, as fast as you can, for sure to come after you, they are, once they find you are gone."

"Will you come with me, Myfanwy?"

"Heavens, no! Only slow you down, I would. No, you just get yourself to Carmarthen and find the station. Have you got money?"

"Yes, but. . . ."

"My bike is parked out by the back door. Take that as far as Brechfa and then you'll find a bus for Carmarthen. You'd better hurry; they might be back in the house at any moment."

"I . . . don't like leaving you here. . . ."

"Never mind about that, now! I'll try to slow them up here as much as I can. If only a train to London you can catch, then you'll be safe from them."

"Will I?" murmured Pandora thoughtfully. "I wonder. . . ." She slipped her hand into her pocket, where the brass key was hidden. She wondered if running would be her best course.

"Come on, now!" urged Myfanwy anxiously. "There is no time for standing around." She took Pandora's arm and hurried her out onto the landing. "They may have stepped out just for a few minutes. . . ."

"Indeed they may," agreed a familiar voice at the foot of the stairs. Pandora and Myfanwy froze, as though turned to stone. Gazing down over the bannister rail, they saw Aunt Rachel and Ewen making their way slowly up the staircase.

Aunt Rachel tutted softly to herself.

"You've been very foolish, Myfanwy," she said, her eyes fixed on the housekeeper in cold accusation. "I am very disappointed in you, though I confess I half expected something like this. That is why Ewen and myself slipped out for a while; to give you the opportunity of playing your hand. This is really very tiresome. . . ."

Myfanwy shook her head defiantly.

"You just stay where you are!" she cried. "I'll not let you harm the girl!"

Aunt Rachel hesitated for a moment. "You'll not let me?" she echoed. "Come now, Myfanwy, there's really very little you can do." She continued to come forward, with Ewen just a step behind her. Myfanwy pushed Pandora back along the landing and pointed an unsteady hand at Aunt Rachel.

"Too long I've stood by and done nothing!" she cried. "I've known about the wickedness in your soul for as long as I can remember; and damned my own soul will be, for sharing such secrets, too. But listen here, Rachel Ellis, they say blood will have blood. You'll pay for your sins before very long, mark my words. And if you want Pandora, you'll have to kill me first!"

Aunt Rachel shrugged expressively.

"My dear Myfanwy," she said matter of factly. "Do you really think I could let you go on living anyway?" She was almost at the top of the stairs now, one gaunt hand reaching out for the rail. Suddenly, Myfanwy leapt forward with a cry and launched herself at the old woman. They collided briefly, grappled, and fell back against Ewen, who came instinctively to his mistress' aid. For a moment the three of them struggled together. Myfanwy's hands were around Aunt Rachel's throat and, for an instant, it looked as though she might succeed in her aim. But then, Ewen got his long, muscled arms around Myfanwy's neck and he dragged her away from her quarry, pushed her back, kicking and struggling, against the bannister rail. Pandora stood looking on in helpless fear. Aunt Rachel turned away from the others, her hand massaging her bruised throat, and then she glanced up at Pandora with eyes that smouldered with hot, black rage.

Pandora backed slowly away along the landing; then, she jumped at the abrupt noise of splintering, tearing wood and a shrill scream of terror. Appalled, she turned to see Myfanwy's body crash with a hideous thud onto the tiled floor far below. From a broken gap in the railing, Ewen stared down impassively.

"Myfanwy!" shrieked Pandora, numb with shock.

The body lay on its back, twitching convulsively. The eyes were wide open, staring upwards in surprise. The lips moved briefly and said in a curious, croaking tone:

"Pandora . . . sssssorry. . . ." The right arm lifted slightly, as though submitting something for inspection. Then, in an instant, death came, clouding the gentle eyes and snatching the arm down to the tiles again. The body was still. A slow crimson stain began to spread beneath the shattered skull. A terrible silence fell on the house.

"It was an accident," murmured Ewen. "The railings broke."

His voice was calm, thoughtful. Pandora's blood turned to ice in her veins.

"It's just as well," observed Aunt Rachel. "She couldn't be trusted anymore." She turned back to Pandora. "And now, my dear," she whispered, "perhaps you would care to accompany me back to your room."

"You murdered her!" Pandora's voice was hoarse with fright and tears were streaming from her eyes. "You . . . you. . . ." She continued to back away, shaking her head from side to side in shocked disbelief.

"Nonsense, Pandora! It was an accident; you saw it yourself. Come along now and rest for a while." She extended an open hand but Pandora shook her head, refused to take it.

"Don't be a little fool! Can't you see that you've lost? What's the use in fighting when you can't possibly win?"

"Perhaps . . . I can," replied Pandora, wiping away the tears with her sleeve. She took the key from her pocket and held it before her.

Aunt Rachel's face changed as dramatically as the sun swamped by a thundercloud. For a few long moments she was speechless with surprise. Then she cried, "Where did you get that?"

"From your room," said Pandora.

"Give it to me, this instant!"

Pandora shook her head.

"Ewen!" Aunt Rachel called over her shoulder. "Ewen, come here, quickly. She's got hold of that damned key. Ewen, come and help me."

"Help yourself!" came the reply.

Aunt Rachel spun around in amazement. "What did you say?"

Ewen was standing down in the hallway, beside Myfanwy's body. He was holding something up to the light, something that hung on a chain, turning and glittering.

"The Goblin charm," he announced. "Myfanwy must have pulled it from your neck in the fight. It was in her hand."

"Oh, no . . . no. . . ." Aunt Rachel's face turned sickly white and her hands flew instinctively to her neck. "Give it back to me," she hissed. "Do you hear me? The charm is mine."

Ewen shook his head, a mocking smile on his lips, "Not any-more," he retorted. "While you wore it, you were strong. I was not able to take the charm from you but another person could. Now you are nothing . . . and I say again, help yourself!" He turned and strolled away, out of their sight.

"Ewen!" screamed Aunt Rachel. "Ewen, damn you! Come back here! She has the key. . . ." She seemed to remember Pandora and she turned back unsteadily. "Pandora," she whispered. "Please . . . just give me the key. We'll talk about everything that's happened here. I'll make you understand why things have to follow a certain path." She began to edge closer but Pandora moved back all the way, glancing off occasionally to where the dusty staircase waited. "Think about it," urged Aunt Rachel. "Perhaps things haven't been happening just as you imagine. . . . We'll talk . . . just you and I. . . ."

She made a swift but clumsy snatch for the key and Pandora evaded her grasp. Turning, she ran for the stairs. Aunt Rachel hurried after her, desperation lending her wings, but Pandora was young and lithe and she hammered up the rickety stairs and through the opening in a few moments, pausing only to switch on the lights at the main socket.

She reached Ellen's door some time before Aunt Rachel did. The key fitted in the lock with a minimum of fuss; all it required now was a single turn. But something made her hesitate for a moment. She turned to face Aunt Rachel as the old woman drew to a halt, a few feet away. She looked totally beaten now, her face white and haggard, her eyes shot through with the cold colour of fear. She was staring at the head of the large, brass key as though nothing else existed in the world. She took an explora-tory step forward, but halted as Pandora lifted her hand to the key.

"No!" she moaned helplessly. "Please, Pandora, don't open the door. You don't know what you are doing!"

"But I do," replied Pandora calmly. "I'm letting Ellen free, and for some reason, that terrifies you. Why?"

"You don't understand! Do you really think that there's a little girl in there?"

"I know there is. I've talked to her."

"*Think*, Pandora! Sixty years . . . how could any little girl survive that long? Believe me, Ellen is dead. What you talked to was . . . a . . . a . . . trick of some kind, that's all."

"If it was a trick, then you've got nothing to fear."

"Please . . . you've got to listen to me. Think of your namesake, Pandora. She opened a box of secrets and was cursed for the rest of time. She got nothing but misery for her pains. . . . You see, that door isn't meant to be opened yet, it's too early. The book says. . . ."

"Don't listen, Pandora!" Ellen's voice came piping in unexpectedly from beyond the door. Aunt Rachel shrank back in undisguised horror.

"There," cried Pandora triumphantly. "She can talk, you see." Again her hand went up to the key.

"Wait!" screamed Aunt Rachel. "Listen to me a moment. . . . I'm a very rich woman, Pandora. There's a certain, secret place in my room where I keep all my money. There's a fortune there, more than you've ever dreamed of . . . if you'll just give me that key. . . ."

"She's trying to trick you!" warned Ellen. "Hurry and open the door. There's not much time."

"But that's not all, Pandora! What about my secret, eh? Wouldn't you like to live forever, never have to worry about dying. . . ?"

Pandora shook her head sadly.

"If it means being like you, Aunt Rachel," she replied, "then I'd just as soon take my chances with the rest."

"Yes, but *think*, Pandora! *THINK!*"

"I don't have to think, Aunt Rachel. I'm sorry, but. . . ."

Suddenly, the old woman was upon her in a desperate, clawing lunge, her sharp fingernails groping for a hold. She slammed Pandora's head back against the door, then flung her roughly to the floor. With a yell of triumph, she reached for and took the key but Pandora was back up in an instant and she grabbed two fistfuls of the old woman's hair and dragged her backwards, to roll and tumble on the dusty floorboards. The key fell from Aunt Rachel's fingers and the two of them scrabbled for possession of it, kicking and hitting at each other blindly. Suddenly, Pandora's hand found cold metal and she rolled away from her Great Aunt and flung herself back to the door. She fumbled the key against the lock several times, giving Aunt Rachel the opportunity to come at her again, but just before she was knocked down for the second time, she managed to slot it into the hole and turn it, with a loud, decisive click.

Then she lay still, panting hoarsely in the terrible silence that followed. Aunt Rachel began to stumble back from the door, her face contorted into a mask of fear. From within the room, there was a strange, mewing cry of exultation and then, suddenly, the door burst open as though smashed by a giant's fist. A hideous, ancient stench of filth and disease came gusting out onto the landing, so powerful that Pandora began to retch. She stared into the dark doorway in horrified fascination, her streaming eyes seeing but not wanting to see the nightmarish figure that lurked there.

It came shuffling painfully out into the glow of electric light. It was roughly the size and shape of a twelve-year-old child; but there the resemblance ended. It was a hideous accumulation of the lines and sores and illnesses of sixty long years, grafted onto the body of a little girl. It was a naked, wizened, leather-skinned dwarf with a face, the features of which had collapsed upon themselves into a portrait of festering ugliness. It was shuffling forward on its short, malformed legs, its arms outstretched as if in greeting, towards the trembling, raving figure of Aunt Rachel.

Pandora screamed, too, as the thing that had been Ellen Hughes wrapped the old woman in a revolting embrace and hugged her close to itself, all the time making little mewing sounds deep in its throat. The air seemed to fill with the acrid smell of sulphur and then, Aunt Rachel's body began to wilt, wither, dry up like an autumn leaf, all in an instant, and suddenly, it was *she* who was aged and decayed and it was a young, fair-haired girl who clung lovingly against her. Aunt Rachel gave one last, feeble wail of despair and then, both her body and that of the child shattered, crumbled and fell into dusty little pieces on the floor. Where the dust fell, a bright, intense fire erupted.

Deep in the grip of nightmare, Pandora yelled for help, half in, half out of reality, and she kept right on yelling as the flames began to blaze through the tinder-dry hallway, eating, devouring everything that existed there and leaving only a myriad far-flung sparks that danced upwards like stars to the waiting rafters.

The blackness that came was soft and warm and restful. There was no reason to fight against it anymore.

She woke from the final nightmare.

She was out in the open and the chilly air of evening was in her lungs. Opening her eyes, she saw Ewen peering down at her. He smiled with relief to see that she was awake. Then he kneeled down and stroked her hair softly.

"Are you all right?" he murmured.

She nodded. "Did you carry me out?"

"Yes. You were very lucky. The old place went up like a matchwood." He gazed off for a moment and his eyes seemed to blaze with yellow light. Pandora realised that she was in the front garden of Savannah and that the house itself was burning from top to bottom, blazing up like a great yellow flower beneath the empty skies. As she watched, part of the roof collapsed, sending up a great cloud of smoke and sparks.

"The bitch is at rest now," muttered Ewen. There was not a trace of compassion in his voice.

"And the charm?" said Pandora.

"I have it here." He held it up for a moment, letting it glitter dangerously in the moonlight. Then he slipped it into his coat pocket. "It will stay with me now," he concluded. "There will be no more slavery." He stood up, helping Pandora to her feet. She stood uncertainly for a moment, still a little dizzy.

"That thing in the room . . . Ellen . . . I never dreamed she would be like that."

"She's free now. Once the house has burned away, there will be nothing to show what happened here."

They both turned to look at the house again. It was now no more than a blackened shell, vomiting its fiery heart up into the air. It had burned very quickly, feeding the flames with the hidden guilt of many lifetimes. Pandora took a long, deep breath. It seemed that, at last, the long mystery was over. Only grey reality remained.

"What happens now?" she asked.

"I shall return to my home," replied Ewen. "There, I shall sleep, until another summons me to walk the earth again." He smiled a peaceful smile. "Only this time, the call will never be made! I will know rest for the first time in over sixty years. I will be free again."

She stared at him.

"But what about me?" she cried.

"You?" He shrugged. "You will go home again," he said, matter of factly. "What has happened here will be put down to an accident. You will never be connected with it."

"But I *love* you!"

He shook his head. "What can you know of love?" he replied. He sounded sad, tired. "You are only a child. It was wrong of me to use you the way I did."

She moved closer to him.

"Let me come with you," she said. "Please."

Again, he shook his head. "It's not possible! You must stay here."

"But I don't understand. You wanted me before . . . and you made me want you."

"I wanted you when I was stranded here, in a land I do not understand or love. Now I can return to the ways I do understand." He glanced quickly around. "Good-bye, Pandora. I'll think of you, sometimes."

"Wait!" She stared at him for a moment. "Please . . . will you kiss me good-bye?"

He smiled, nodded. He reached out and encircled her with his arms, crushing her against his powerful body. For a brief instant their lips touched and she felt the same rush of desire dance through her that she had experienced before. Then, he released her and without a further word, he turned and sprinted away along the drive, in the direction of the forest. He ran fast, never glancing back, and soon he had vanished into the darkness.

"Going home," thought Pandora. She stood gazing along the path, a curious, half-smile written on her lips. She was suddenly aware of a soft footfall behind her. Turning, she saw Geraint standing there, his face a mask of outrage.

"You kissed him," he said numbly. "I saw you kiss him."

"So I did," she replied coolly. She examined Geraint curiously for a moment. "How long have you been around?"

"Half the day! Worried sick about you, I was. What the hell has been going on here?"

"I'll tell you on the way to the police station."

"Pandora? What's the matter with you? You seem *different*."

"Different?" she mused thoughtfully. "Well . . . perhaps I have changed in some ways. It's a long story, really. . . ."

She wondered how much of the truth she should tell him. She gazed at him fondly for a moment, remembering that only a few days ago he had meant something to her. It would only hurt him to know everything that had happened. After all, he was a mere boy.

She took his hand now and they turned and walked along the drive, away from the last burning embers of Savannah. They did not even notice the two pale figures that watched from beneath the shadow of the trees; one, a naked boy, with oddly staring eyes; the other, a pretty fair-haired girl, free from her prison for the first time in many years.

The evening was descending rapidly now and it was a long, cold walk to the village of Brechfa.

Chapter Eighteen

Paddington station seemed more like an ant hill than ever. Samantha and John waited on the crowded platform in a state of nervous agitation.

"Where the hell is it?" snapped John impatiently.

Samantha shook her head. "We should never have let her go. Never!"

They were both irritable and tired; they had been snatched from their sleep in the early hours by a telephone call from the Brechfa police station. There had been a terrible accident at Aunt Rachel's house, a fire that had killed the old woman and a middle-aged housekeeper. Police were on the lookout for the gardener who, they felt, might have been able to help with their enquiries. Pandora, thankfully, was safe and well, though it was not altogether clear how she had managed to escape the blaze. They had talked to Pandora on the phone and she had seemed perfectly calm and collected. John had wanted to drive to Wales there and then but she would have no such thing. She would spend the night at the police station and travel up on the train the following day. She had insisted on this. There was absolutely nothing to worry about.

"Poor little kid," murmured John thoughtfully. "She's a brave one, though. What a rotten experience for her. . . . Make a damn good book."

Samantha glared at him. "For God's sake, John!"

"Sorry. . . ." He stiffened. "Ah . . . here it comes now, I think."

They hurried forward as the train idled its way into the station.

"I don't see her, John!" cried Samantha. "Surely she couldn't have missed it. . . ."

The train lurched to a halt and they hurried along the length of it, systematically checking the windows. And suddenly, there she was, climbing down from an open doorway, waving cheerfully to them. They hesitated for a moment before running to her, because both of them were surprised by the inexplicable change in her appearance. It was as though in the brief week of her absence, she had aged several years. There was a new air of authority in her somehow, the experienced glint of confidence in her eyes that came across at a single glance . . . and though it was impossible, it seemed to Samantha that her daughter's tomboyish figure had blossomed into attractive feminine curves. She had gone away a child and returned a woman . . . and yet there was something more to it than that . . . an inexplicable darkness beneath the girl's eyes. A hint of suggestion in her smile. A vague offhandedness as she parried the barrage of inevitable questions.

"Are you all right, darling?"

"I'm fine, Mummy."

"How on earth did the fire start?"

"I'm not sure, Daddy. The policeman thought it might have been a paraffin stove or something."

"Poor Aunt Rachel . . . we'll never know what she was like, now. . . . What did you think of her?"

"She was . . . very interesting."

Pandora looked from one parent to the other with calm deliberation as they talked to her, realising that although she herself might have changed in some ways, they most certainly had not. Smiling, she reached out and took one of their hands in each of her own, pulling them towards the ticket gate. Her path seemed perfectly clear now. She would guide them from here onwards and the journey would be of her making. She was strong enough now to make them see the error of their ways.

She wondered if her parents could sense the change in her.   I 44

She herself could sense it growing, hour by hour, gnawing deep inside her like a powerful, craving hunger. She had no qualms about what she had done. Ewen should have realised that she wanted him too much ever to let him go.

"Oh, darling, how lovely! Wherever did you get it from?"

"It was a present from someone, Mummy."

"It's beautiful. Whoever gave you such a lovely thing?"

"A . . . young man. He was kissing me good-bye and he almost forgot to leave it with me. Would you believe that I had to pick his pocket?"

"Romancer! It is nice, though. I wouldn't be surprised if it's real silver. Goodness, look how it glitters! I must say, I hope that this young man pays us a visit before too long."

Pandora smiled strangely and gave the Goblin charm a squeeze.

"I expect he'll be along," she replied. "I hardly see how he'll be able to stay away. Come on, let's go home."

Laughing, the three of them walked out of the station, into the grey chill of morning.